Missing

Ron Mueller

<u>**Fiction Series**</u>

The Alex Evercrest Series
The River Front
The Girl on The Grill
Missing
Maggot
Racist
Votive Candles
Windy City
Country Road
Pool of Blood
Sins of the Daughter
Body Parts
The Skull Collector
The Vanishing
The Shadow Fighter
Moonshine
Grief's Trajectory
The Magic Touch
Northern Lights
Alex Evercrest Heroine
Alex Evercrest Collection Two
New Direction
A Family Affair
Disruption
The St. Lebuinnus Church Murder

A Brian O'Neil Novel
Hawaiian Phoenix
Moon Curser
Death Broker

The Problem Solver Series
Solutions
Drug Lords
Border Crosser
The Problem Solver Collection

<u>The Taelo Series</u>
Taelo: The Early Years
Taelo: The Golden Feather
Taelo: Journey of Discovery
Taelo: Dangerous Passage
Taelo: Condor Clan Slingers
Taelo: Circumvention
Taelo: The Journey of Sages
Taelo: Collection
Taelo: Future Leaders Journey

<u>A Taelo Story:</u>
White Swan and Quiet Pheasant
The Child's Name
Floating Cloud
Quiet Rabbit
Busy Bee
Little Otter & Talking Wren
Broken Spear
Burley Bear & Meadow Flower
Taelo Story Collection

Ron Mueller

<u>Science Fiction</u>
The Savitar Series:
Journey's End
Savitar
Confluence
Savitar Series Collection

Bram Nielson Series
The Fold
The Message
Fold Wormhole
Negative Fold
Ripples in Time
Bram Nielson Collection

<u>Single Science Fiction Books:</u>
Current Past and Future
The Event
The Door
Viajante 7

Missing

By: *Ron Mueller*

Around the World Publishing LLC
Cincinnati, Ohio

Ron Mueller

Missing, Copyright ©

ISBN 13: 978-1-68223-331-3

Distributed by Ingram
Alex Evercrest Model By: Pi03@ShutterStock
Cincinnati Scene: Nagel Photography @ShutterStock
Cover Design By: Ron Mueller

Dedicated to those families who have suffered by Missing sons, daughters and loved ones.

<u>Table of Contents</u>

1. Cold Case by a Hand From Above   1

2. The Sheriff's Albatross   11

3. The Clue   29

4. The Parents   39

5. Annie   49

6. Explosive Verification   61

7. The Cabin   71

8. Jeff   83

9. Found   95

10. Home   105

11. Once in a Lifetime   115

12. Dessert   135

13. The Mall   143

14. Dinner   151

15. The Meaning of Survival   163

16. Future   171

Preview of: Maggot   175

About the Author   199

Books by the Author   200

1 Cold Case by a Hand from Above

Alex and Trey, her detective partner were back in Cincinnati after pursuing a lunatic person in Mississippi. This person had destroyed Alex's apartment with a rocket propelled grenade. They had almost been shot by this person with a shotgun during her apprehension and later at the local hospital this same woman managed to escape from her hospital bed, take a policeman's gun, and shoot at Alex. Alex's swift reflex and deadly aim ended the confrontation with the woman face down on the floor from a shot to the chest and one between her eyes.

During that case, Alex had survived two attacks in her own Cincinnati apartment.

The first was the rocket propelled grenade, launched by the lunatic that Alex had ultimately killed in Mississippi, had demolished her first apartment.

The second attack was on her return from Mississippi. The drug distributor involved in the case had gained access to her new apartment by climbing externally up two floors to her exterior apartment porch.

She had picked up a suitor in Mississippi that had followed her to Cincinnati. He was the EMT that she had met in Mississippi. His unexpected knock on her apartment door, when she was being held at gun point, had given her the opportunity to get help.

She had told him to go away and that solicitors were not allowed in the building. He had figured out that something was wrong. He called the Cincinnati Chief of police and asked for help. When help arrived and was breaking down the door, Alex dived at the intruder as he shot at her. In the ensuing struggle the intruder was shot by his own gun. He survived.

She had shot and killed two people in less than a month. Her swift actions and her swift and deadly shooting had earned her the handle of "the Cincinnati's Black Annie Oakley."

Alex leaned back in her chair and took in the few detectives that were currently sitting at their desks.

She and Trey were both stressed out.

He had moved to Cincinnati to get away from the stress of a similar situation during his tenure as a policeman in Milwaukee. Before taking a job in the Milwaukee police department, he had survived Afghanistan. He knew he had a case of PTSD, and he was also enrolled in Alcoholics Anonymous with Alex.

Trey recognized that he was now partnered at work with a person that seemed to be a magnet for violence but who had gotten him help with his dependence on alcohol, who had become a close family friend and who was adored by his son, Nolan.

He knew he would have a lifetime of managing the stress, but he had a work partner that he could look to for help, an adoring beautiful wife, and a son to greet him after each day's work.

A few days after their return from Mississippi, Johnnie, the old Vietnam veteran that Alex had recruited to work for her, and the police department had surprised both of them by coming into the office. He was excited and said he had the perfect case for them to handle. He was sure Alex could solve a long-standing cold case about a missing girl. He had gotten interested in her when the local news had highlighted the fifteenth anniversary of her disappearance. He had used his investigative skills on his personal computer and on the office police computer. He was sure he had some new leads for Alex to follow.

Alex thanked him and slowly reviewed his report. As always, Johnnie had a solid, thorough in-depth report. It was clear this case had somehow caught his interest because he had done an analysis of every individual mentioned in the original police report. The mother and father of the missing child still lived in Cincinnati Area.

The mother worked at a major food store. The father was a truck driver. They had two additional children ages nine and seven. It sounded like a case she might someday look into. She again thanked Johnnie but said she was not ready to dig into the case at the moment.

Johnnie let out a small groan and looked disappointed, but he said he would wait until she was ready. Then he would help her in any way possible. He got up and said he would see the two of them later.

Alex and Trey had been promised a couple of easy weeks by the Cincinnati's Chief of detectives, Bruce Johnson, and he had delivered but he was now beckoning the two of them into his office.

Oh no, escaped from her mouth as she stood up.

Trey had heard her exclamation and just said Ditto.

The Chief's office door leading to the detective work area had been left open and Alex followed by Trey walked slowly toward it in an apprehensive way. The hair on the back of her neck had automatically stood up when the Chief signaled to them. She hoped that he remembered that he had promised to go easy on the two of them for a few weeks.

As she and Trey walked in, Alex looked at the chief and then took in the mild-mannered woman with black hair sitting stiffly upright in the chair in front of the chief's desk. The woman seemed nervous. Alex noted that the woman's her right hand kept clenching her left hand.

Alex let Trey go past her then closed the door. She took in the scene and noted Bruce's nod for her to sit down.

The Chief introduced the woman as Martha Melville a librarian in the Cincinnati Library. He wanted Alex to listen to the story that Martha had to tell.

Alex asked if Martha happened to know Johnnie Lancaster. Martha smiled and said that if he was a black Vietnam veteran that constantly frequented the library and managed to get a few cookies from attending various presentation, then she knew Johnnie.

Alex shared that she had hired him as a computer analyst and had gotten him a job as a super for her apartment building.

Martha smiled and said that explained why she had seen less of Johnnie.

Alex noted that this simple interchange had changed the atmosphere in the room. Martha now seemed to relax as she leaned back in her chair.

The Chief asked Martha to tell her story to Alex and Trey.

Alex listened as Martha recalled the story of Annie Lorie Scots a young girl that had gone missing and had never been found. Martha told of an acquaintance that had told her of a young woman being held in the woods in southern New York state. The timing of the rumors and stories told about the situation seemed to coincide with Annie's disappearance. Martha's informant had not given her the name of the neighbor or the location where Annie might be.

Alex asked for a moment so she could get some information that had been given to her just a few days ago.

Alex walked out and retrieved Johnnie's report. She pulled it from her file and walked back into the office.

Alex asked Martha if she knew anything about Annie's parents.

Martha said she had done a little bit of an investigation on her own. The parents were library members and had two girls that were also members. She said she had written down some of the information that she had dug up.

After rummaging for moment through her purse she pulled out a folded sheet of paper and put it on the desk.

Alex thanked her and leaned forward to read the information on the paper. She was stunned when it matched the one in Johnnie's report.

She thanked Martha and told her that she would be looking into the case. She set up a time that she could speak to Martha at the library.

The Chief escorted Martha out to the front door and thanked her for coming forward. He stood and watched as Martha walked out in the direction of the library.

He was taken aback by the fact that Alex had a quarter inch thick report on a case that he knew nothing about. He then turned and hurried back to his office. He wanted to know how Alex had a report on this specific case.

Alex had relaxed and quietly asked Trey to relax until the Chief came back. She knew he would want to know how she had a report on a cold case without his knowledge. She told Trey she would handle the Chief.

The Chief entered his office looked at Alex and asked her to clue him in. He asked how she had gotten the files of a cold case without him knowing it?

Alex explained that it was not an official police cold case file but a report that Johnnie had given her a few days ago. It had been his intention to give her an easy job. He had gotten into the case because of a Cincinnati television station that reported on the fifteenth anniversary on Annie's disappearance.

The Chief took the report and quickly flipped through it. He looked at Alex and asked if she and Trey were ready to get back to work and that he was assigning her to look into and solve the cold case. He said that to him it was no coincident that both Johnnie and Martha the librarian had come forward with the same case. To him it was a biblical sign, and he was going to make an official opening of Annie's cold case.

Alex walked out to the copy machine and made a copy of Johnnie's report. She returned and gave the Chief a copy. She told him to read it slowly and that it would raise the hair on the back of his neck and maybe put some hair on top of his head.

He gruffly told her to get to work. Personally, he had confidence that Alex would get to the bottom of the case. He gave a small prayer that she would do it without the fireworks and shootings of the last case.

She gave a salute and walked back to her desk.

She called Johnnie and asked if he would like to sit in as she and Trey developed a plan to look into the case, he had brought to her.

She suggested his apartment as the meeting place if he would provide coffee. The alternative would be the station and station house coffee.

Johnnie chose his apartment and offered to have some donuts or fruit. Alex replied that a banana would do.

She and Trey walked eight blocks to her apartment building where both she and Johnnie lived. She knocked on Johnnie's apartment door and was quickly taken in.

The first thing Johnnie asked was why she had changed her mind about taking up the cold case.

Alex joked with him and told him that she had seen tears in his eyes and had felt so bad that she told Trey they would have to do it.

Johnnie knew immediately that Alex was joking with him and said that he had another tougher case handy if she was interested.

She told Johnnie about Martha's visit to the station and the fact that her information built on the research Johnnie had done. Martha had been the catalyst in getting the cold case recognized but that his research was what opened it.

Johnnie let out a low whistle. He commented that the investigation had an invisible hand guiding it.

Alex smiled and shook her head up and down as she agreed with him. She commented that the Chief had said the same thing when he declared he was opening up Annie's cold case. She commented that a cold shiver had run down her back when she had listened to Martha and it had just done so again. She commented that this was a cold case that she was determined to solve.

She also joked that the Martha had remembered Johnnie as a regular cookie thief.

Johnnie gave a small laugh and confessed that he had scrounged many a cookie by attending presentation sessions at the Library. It had been a dry, safe, and enjoyable place for him. He said that he would have to bake some cookies and take them to the library as a thank-you gesture.

The plan of how to get into the cold case slowly took shape. Alex asked Johnnie to do some additional on-line searches that might be needed. She and Trey would interview Martha again and go over everything they had to date.

She had identified the person who had closed the case. He was now the sheriff in Loveland. She planned to get him to take a lead role in looking into the case.

They would also see if they could interview the mother and father of the missing girl.

Alex closed the planning session and declared she was going to work out in the Gym. She told Trey to go home early and enjoy the last day of taking it easy.

She suggested they meet the following day at the station. They would begin by setting up appointments with Martha and the Loveland Sheriff.

Johnnie said that he would do the research that Alex had requested.

Alex had a surge of energy that came from the interaction she had with her team. Her team that functioned so smoothly, so efficiently, effectively and was becoming unstoppable. She hoped that they would break the cold case wide open.

Later she would learn that her hopes would be well short of the miracle that awaited but would take her into a lifelong relationship.

2 The Sheriff's Albatross

Alex sat in her bed and read over Johnnies' report on Annie. She carefully and thoroughly went through what had happened to Annie. It was 1987 when Annie Scots went out to play with a neighbor. Not much later the neighbor called to ask when Annie was coming over. Annie's mother immediately went out and looked for Annie. She was never found.

For days and weeks, the local news and a few national channels featured the parent's pleas for the return of their daughter. The pleas went unanswered and soon the coverage ended.

The Loveland police department kept the case open for five years. They questioned all neighbors and checked several of them out but had gotten no viable leads.

A yearly plea was still put out by her parents.

Alex got up and Googled Loveland.

In its early days, Loveland was known as a resort town, with its summer homes for the wealthy, earning it the nickname "Little Switzerland of the Miami Valley." It became known for being extremely safe with a very low crime rate and a family friendly community.

She found the downtown area of Loveland to be charming. It had family-friendly restaurants, a park and the Loveland bike trail that ran from downtown Cincinnati past Loveland for some hundred miles. Alex had ridden through Loveland several times when she went on her long bike rides.

Loveland was about twenty-five miles by car from headquarters.

It can't happen here was erased by Annie's disappearance.

To Alex this incident reinforced her belief that bad things happened in the best communities.

The next morning, as usual she biked to work. Her first stop after changing into her work outfit was the coffee machine. She was greeted by Bill and Travis who were sitting having coffee and a donut. Bill lifted the donut box and offered her one. She thanked him but shook her head to indicate she was passing on the offer.

Trey walked in a few moments later with his coffee in hand. He accepted the offer of a donut.

After a few moments of the four of them chatting, Trey led the way to one of the huddle rooms.

From there she called the Loveland Police office and set up an interview with their Sheriff. Years ago, he was the young deputy that had closed Annie's case. He agreed to an interview but voiced his doubts about having any success in solving the case. She said that his information and recall was critical, and he might have an insight and know nuances that would not be in a written report. She wanted to interview him before interviewing Annie's parents. She figured it was a necessary step of reopening the case that he had closed as a rooky police officer.

Alex was surprised at the initial response from the sheriff. He seemed offended that the Cincinnati police department was opening up his cold case.

She put out an invitation for him to become part of the team. She knew that if he felt threatened, he might turn into the worst of adversaries. This was something she did not need.

The Scots, Annie's parents, still lived in Loveland. They were second on Alex's list as she set out to learn more about that fateful day.

Alex knew that usually abductions were done by someone close to the family. She planned to ask Johnny to apply his computer skills to learn all he could about relatives and neighbors. She was especially interested in any that lived along the border of New York state and northern Pennsylvania or had property there.

She was personally planning to interview every person that had lived in Annie's neighborhood and still lived there. She would interview every relative that had been in the area when Annie disappeared. She was trying to control her bias about it being a male abductor. This was hard to do since more than eighty percent of abductions were by a male relative or someone close to the family.

Loveland Sheriff Evan Williams sat looking at the phone. He wondered why the Cincinnati Police were opening up Annie's cold case. He decided he wanted to know more and put in a call to one of his old buddies that was in the same office as the detective that had just called him.

He listened as his buddy Travis described the detective, he was curious about as "Cincinnati's black Annie Oakley." He was surprised at Travis's enthusiastic support of a female police officer. This Alex Evercrest must be a powerful presence. The fact that she had overcome multiple extremely violent personal attacks gave him some hope that she would solve the case that had haunted him throughout his career.

He hung up and called for Annie's cold case documents. He had not looked at them for several years and he wanted to refresh his memory. He always had bad memories when he reviewed the case. He considered it one of his top failures.

He decided that the best action was to first take a short bike ride along the Loveland bike trail and have a good lunch at his favorite sandwich shop. The ride would refresh him and give him new energy to once again relive the past that seemed like only yesterday. Once he got back, he would review the case that had been an albatross around his neck for his entire career.

Meanwhile Alex had invited Trey and Johnnie to have lunch at their favorite lunch spot. This was the restaurant where Alex had shot and killed the person who had thrown the young lady off an overpass onto the grill of a semitruck. This killer had made the mistake of confronting her and pulling a gun that he never got to use because Alex put a bullet into his forehead as he brought the gun out from its holster.

As she and her partner, Trey, got into the car she took a few moments to check that he was OK in her getting the both of them into Annie's cold case. She had become good friends with Trey. They both went to the same AA group each week. She often went to family dinners with Trey, his wife, and his son. She knew how the stress of getting into this case was already affecting her. She wanted to make sure Trey was OK.

Trey admitted that it did increase his stress but that for him it was different than before. He praised her for being a partner that recognized the stress but kept her cool. It inspired him and made things easier.

Alex thanked him and then led the way into the restaurant. She had gone there often enough that many of the staff knew her and always took her to the seat that she had when she had been attacked.

After lunch Alex took Trey up on his request to drive to Loveland. They had been issued a new car, and this was his first time to drive it.

She said she wanted to stop and buy some Toblerone and Ghirardelli chocolate on sale at Costgood. It would be a short stop on the way to Loveland.

When Trey asked what she had in mind, Alex replied that her mother had always told her that "you catch more flies with honey than with anything else."

Trey looked at her and replied that he would watch and figure it out.

She took the car's instruction book out of the glove compartment and read about the operating features. She learned that the car could be started remotely. This would be a nice feature on cold days.

Alex dozed for a few minutes but came to full attention when Trey exited 71 and proceeded to Costco.

Alex went in and bought three pentagon boxes of Toblerone and three bags of Ghirardelli chocolate. On the way back to the car she told Trey how to start the car remotely. She also told him how to roll down the windows remotely.

She directed Trey to follow Union Cemetery Road toward Loveland.

A few moments later, Alex took in the Police building and expressed her opinion that the architect had used the windows to make the exterior look like the bars of a prison cell. The large parking lot was edged by a well-kept hedge and was almost totally empty. Parking would be no problem.

Sheriff Evan Williams watched as the car pulled into the parking lot. He knew immediately that it was a Cincinnati unmarked police car.

He closed Annie's file and checked to see that he had a fresh pot of coffee ready.

Trey chose the parking spot closest to the entrance.

Alex took one box and one bag of the chocolates and led the way in. Inside they were greeted by a tough looking deputy that sat behind an elevated counter. Alex and Trey both showed him their badge.

The deputy asked if they were armed.

Both Alex and Trey responded that they were.

The sergeant momentarily turned off the metal detector and had them enter.

Alex and Trey followed the deputy's instruction.

She stopped as she exited the scanner. She looked at the deputy and told him he needed a little sweetening. She gave him the five bar Toblerone box and asked him to share it with the other folks.

She took in his surprised look and his smile and quiet thank you.

She and Trey then turned to follow his instructions.

A female deputy met them as they turned toward the sheriff's office. She introduced herself as Melony and greeted them. She asked them to follow her to the chief's office.

Alex sensed that the escort by a female deputy was an intentional display by the Loveland sheriff. She asked Melony how long she had been on the force. Melony replied that the sheriff had hired her three years ago. Alex inferred that her guide was a signal by the sheriff that he supported equal treatment.

Alex was immediately on alert. She knew the sheriff had sounded unhappy that "his" cold case was being reopened by someone other than himself.

She was intent on enrolling him and making him a partner in the upcoming search for closure in Annie's case. She wanted to have his support and be on the resolution team. She did not want him to be a barrier.

Sheriff Williams stood up and took in the young black and good-looking detective and her partner. He was immediately captured by her composure and her greeting and her extended hand in which she held a bag of Ghirardelli chocolate. He wondered if she knew that these were one of his favorite chocolates.

He chuckled and asked whether he needed sweetening. He liked her immediately.

He stepped around his desk and shook her hand and then the hand of her partner. He was curious and ready to listen to what she had to say.

Alex looked over at the coffee pot and asked if she might get a cup. Trey said he would love one as well.

She watched as the sheriff took three plain white mugs and poured the coffee. She took her cup and then sat down on one of the chairs in front of the sheriff's desk. Trey did likewise.

The Sheriff took his mug in both hands and looked at Alex and asked why Annie's case was being reopened and why he had not been notified before its reopening.

Alex expressed the fact that if she were in his shoes she would probably be upset. She went on to explain that she had just finished with a trying case and had really been looking forward to a couple of months of boredom. She shared the fact that her on-line investigator had given her an analysis on Annie that he thought she should investigate. She had turned him down. Then a few hours later her Chief had called her into the office to listen to a Cincinnati Librarian about a young woman being held captive in the mountains in either northern Pennsylvania or southern New York. It was almost immediately clear that the story given to her by her analyst and that of the librarian were one and the same.

She shared that she had agreed with her Chief's opinion that having two sources identify the same case in the same week was a sign from above that she should look into the case.

Alex stopped for a moment and then expressed her desire for the Sheriff to be an integral part of the investigation. Alex pointed out that he might remember details that were not on the official report. He had lived it whereas she had to dig through paperwork to establish some connection and context for the case.

She specifically said she felt that his partnership would have a significant positive impact and help in finding out what happened and help solve the case.

Sheriff Williams looked at Alex for a long time. He had been surprised by her explanation about why the cold case was being opened. At that moment he felt hope that at long last the case would be solved.

He felt a shiver run down his back.

He looked at Alex and explained how this case had been an albatross around his neck. It had haunted him for his entire career. Every year he contacted Annie's family to see how they were doing.

He admitted that he had been offended that someone else had decided to open up his cold case. He went on to say that Alex's invitation for him to participate convinced him that she was the right person to take a crack at closing the case.

He voiced his doubts but said he would be on her side.

Alex thanked the sheriff for the compliment and went on to ask him to review the case.

She asked him to go step by step, day by day through the case. She was sure there would be additional information that had not been in the report.

She also asked the sheriff to arrange interviews with Annie's parents and with each of the neighbors.

The sheriff asked her to call him Evan and agreed to set up the visits with everyone in the neighborhood.

Alex immediately sensed the emotional impact the case had on the sheriff. As he recalled the incident and added depth to the report, his voice often quavered, and it seemed that he periodically got tears in his eyes. He had been describing the events for almost an hour when he asked if they could take a break. He said he needed to get outside for some fresh air. He invited Alex and Trey to go with him.

The sheriff led them to a tan SUV and invited them to take a drive with him. Alex and Trey looked at each other and then accepted the invitation.

The interior of the SUV had light brown leather seats and was immaculate and had the smell of a brand-new car.

Alex commented on the the quality of the ride.

The sheriff chuckled and thanked her and commented that the car was his wife's car. He said that he drove a forteen year old Honda Accord that was in the shop for its one hundred forty thousand mile tune up. He commented that he had splurged on new tires at Costgood.

The sheriff drove to the down town district. He parked the car in the street in front of his favorite Grill. He looked at Alex and asked if she wanted to take a walk. He didn't wait for a response but started a slow walk toward the river.

Alex wasn't sure where the little adventure was taking her but she agreed as she got out of the car. The Sheriff led the way back along Loveland Avenue until he got to the bridge. He walked to the center and looked down to the Little Miami river.

He looked at Alex and commented that he came to this spot almost everyday and almost everyday he thought of Annie. Alex listened as he went on tell her that every time someone drove by and honked their horn and waved, it saved him from the remorse he felt about that long cold case.

He said he would do everything possible to help her close it.

As if on que, a car drove past and honked their horn.

The sheriff smiled and asked if the two of them were ready for a cup of coffee at the Grill.

He led the way back and led the way in.

Alex came to a stop as she absorbed the atmosphere. A hand-written sign welcoming the customer was at the end of the counter closest to the door. A guitar enclosed in a glass covered wooden case was mounted on the wall above the bar at the far end. She knew of the Loveland bike trail and wondered what the two bicycles with white lights mounted on the wall signified.

A series of pictures and paintings led her eyes from the red bicycle up on the wall to an area to her right where additional paintings and pictures decorated the walls. A small wooden boat with oars was the final item that caught her attention. After taking it all in she proceeded to the eight-sided black topped table where the sheriff and Trey were sitting. She liked the feel of the place.

The sheriff commented that the Grill always had an impact on him too.

Coffee was ordered and Alex turned down the offer of a donut and opted for a banana.

The sheriff commented that he was burnt out on the interview about Annie but would make additional notes to share. He went on to say that he had not made his annual visit to Annie's parents and that he would arrange to do so. He invited both Alex and Trey to come with him.

Alex had accomplished what she had set out to do. Sheriff Evan Williams was now on her team, and he was taking the action that she needed him to.

The ride back to the Loveland police station was a quiet one. It was clear to Alex that they were all affected by the case.

A few moments later the Sheriff parked next to her car. He looked over at her and commented that he had his mind on some Ghirardelli chocolate and asked if she wanted one before leaving.

Alex thanked him and let him know that she had also bought a bag for she and Trey.

She remarked that it would be great to get to talk to Annie's parents as soon as possible. She also requested his assistance in getting interviews set up with all the neighbors around and behind Annie's home.

He replied that he had accepted the chocolates because they were his favorites and he now he realized she had succeeded in bribing him. After a small chuckle, he said he would make the arrangements with Annie's parents and each of the neighbors that had lived there at the time when Annie went missing.

Alex commented that the candy approach was her mother's idea and that her mother got smarter with each passing year.

She shook the sheriff's hand and welcomed him onto the cold case solution team.

He replied that he would see her soon and that he felt they would make a good team.

She turned and opened the door to her car as Trey got into the driver's seat.

Trey commented that the meeting with the sheriff had been a resounding success. He complimented her in the chocolate candy approach and said he would push for her handle to be 'Cincinnati's sweet Annie Oakley."

Alex replied that he had done enough in getting her labeled as the black Annie Oakley and he should leave well enough alone. She then dialed Martha, the librarian, and set up a meeting at two.

Trey commented that she seemed to be moving fast.

Alex replied that she intended to dig as deep as possible as quickly as possible. She said she felt that the person responsible might react negatively and she did not want to give that person time to react. She wanted that person to panic and make mistakes.

She suggested they stop at the Cheesecake Factory for lunch. She made the point that it was her treat. She knew that Trey was trying to stay on a tight budget because he was saving to buy a house.

Trey thanked her and told her that he owed her. He invited her to a Sunday lunch at his house. He knew his son, Nolan, enjoyed playing with Alex.

His wife, Leslie, was also fond of Alex. She credited Alex with helping him get control of his drinking habit. He also credited Alex.

He had turned her down when she had first invited him to join her in her visits to her AA meetings, but she always let him know when she was attending the meeting and asked if he would like to as well.

She had never pressured him, but he finally realized that she would continue to invite him until he at least went once.

Alex had not pushed but always let him know when she was attending the meeting. Her approach worked.

He spontaneously agreed to go with her a few weeks after many invitations. They now attended the meetings together on a regular basis. He found that the meetings and his partnership with Alex both contributed to his staying sober.

Alex accepted his invitation to a Sunday dinner at his place and responded that she would buy the desert of his choice at the Cheesecake Factory if he would let her have a spoonful.

Too soon a great lunch was over, and Alex had her spoonful. They headed back to the station.

The next stop on their way back was the Library.

Trey parked the car on the street and followed Alex into the Library. He took note that she was again carrying a bag of Ghirardelli candy.

They went to the main desk at the entrance and inquired about Martha. They were told to take the elevator to the third floor. Martha would be waiting for them and would lead them to her office.

Alex greeted Martha and gave her the chocolates after a brief hug. It was immediately apparent that Martha was touched and pleased as she volunteered that Ghirardelli chocolates were one of her favorite weaknesses.

Martha led them back behind the third-floor reference desk to a small office where she opened her gift and offered them a choice of the gold, black, blue, or brown wrapped Ghirardelli. She picked one of the gold wrapped ones for herself.

Alex took a black wrapped one which she knew was plain dark chocolate. Trey took a blue wrapped one. The focus on the candy allowed Alex to lead the way into the discussion about Annie.

Martha recounted her story and as she went along, she remembered that the person who had shared the story about a mysterious cabin in the mountains had mentioned that it was north of the Pennsylvania finger lakes.

This piece of information excited Alex. She knew that Johnnie would be able to use the location to see if anyone in Annie's neighborhood had any property in that area. She knew that this information might be the big break she was looking for.

As she thought about this possibility, she finally opened her Ghirardelli and let the sweet dark chocolate melt slowly in her mouth.

Martha continued her story, but she still could not remember the name of the person who had told her the story. She apologized and pointed out that she talked to dozens of people a day and it seemed each had some personal story they wished to share. She confessed that on somedays she would walk between the book stacks hiding from the library patrons so that she did not need to listen to them.

Alex thanked her for the chocolate and the information. She made the point that the Finger Lake location was a very valuable clue that she was eager to explore. If it led somewhere, she promised to let Martha know.

As they left the Library, Alex suggested that they go and meet with Johnnie at his apartment and bring him up to date on what they had learned.

Her reliance on, Johnnie and his keen ability to cruise the internet and harvest the seeds that people had planted continued to grow. It was a relationship that was paying forward. She had put him on solid ground. He would for the rest of his time repay that by keeping her on that same solid footing.

<u>3 The Clue</u>

*T*he drive from the library to the apartment building where both she and Johnnie lived was only five blocks but to Alex it seemed to take longer than the drive had been out to Loveland. She felt that she had the breakthrough clue. She was certain that Johnnie and his talent for surfing the internet and digging up information would help her solve Annie's cold case.

It was hard for her not to speed as she drove.

Her vision of Annie's fate was frightening, horrific and yet if her vision was the correct one there was a silver lining, Annie would still be alive! Alex imagination kept running through the various scenarios by which Annie might still be alive and in what condition she might be. It gnawed at her psyche.

As soon as the car was parked and the engine off, she jumped out and almost ran to the entrance. She remembered that Trey was with her, so she waited at the buildings entrance door.

He asked why she was so excited.

She just waved him in and then went around him and almost ran to Johnnie's apartment.

A moment after her knock, Johnnie opened the door. He took one look at her face and blurted out, "You got a clue, or have you solved the case without my help.

"I have a great clue, and you are going to turn it into gold," Alex replied as she gave him her usual hug.

Trey walked in behind the two and closed the door. He wanted to know why Alex had not clued him in about the clue.

She looked at him and replied that he had been sitting next to her when Martha shared the biggest lead that had so far come up. She went on to say that she had been hoping for such a clue to come up during their interview with the Sheriff.

It was Martha that had caused the reopening of the cold case, and it was Martha that had the clue.

Johnnie poured out three cups of coffee and then looked at Alex and asked her if she planned to share this great clue.

Alex was quiet for a moment and then stated that if the story that Martha had shared was true Annie might well still be alive. She stopped and looked at Trey and Johnnie to see what their reaction to her statement might be.

Trey raised an eyebrow as he took a sip of coffee. He then said that he doubted she could still be alive. He looked at Alex and stated that was almost never the pattern of the abduction or disappearance of a young girl.

Johnnie put his hand on her arm and said that he believed her. He went on to ask why she had come to him. He wanted to know what she wanted of him.

Alex looked at Trey and as she went on, she handed him a gold Ghirardelli chocolate and accompanied it by saying she was going to demonstrate the power of her intuition and belief in miracles.

She looked at Johnnie and replied that she wanted him to solve Annie's cold case and help bring her home alive.

Johnnie looked at Trey and commented that he must be hearing things wrong. He asked Trey if Alex had just asked him to solve the case and shook his head.

In an intense manner Alex commented that if the story shared by Martha had any truth in it then there was a good chance that Annie was alive somewhere north of the Finger Lake area of Pennsylvania.

She wanted Johnnie to find out if anyone in the Loveland neighborhood where Annie had lived had any property along the New York State and Pennsylvania border.

Johnnie said he would do a thorough search of every one of Annie's neighbors. He went on to say that he doubted that anyone owned property in the Finger Lakes area that would be in their name. He made the point that such connection would have been noted during a police investigation of the neighbors.

Alex said she understood but she went on to ask that he investigate every neighbor and dig into their family connections and locations. She said she felt certain that there was a connection somewhere.

Almost a week went by. Every morning, she would stop and check on Johnnie's progress and encouraged him to dig deeper.

She had updated the Chief and shared her view that Annie might still be alive. He commented that it would be a miracle if she were.

To that statement she reminded him that he was the one that said a hand from above had something to do with opening Annie's cold case. She went on to say that perhaps that hand was still making things happen.

Alex refused to give up the hope that Annie was still alive, but time weighed heavy on her.

Sheriff Williams's call asking if she were available to meet with Annie's parents the next day lifted her emotions from the bottom of the bucket.

The sheriff went on to let her know that he had contacted all the neighbors that had lived there when Annie lived there and had arranged meetings with them as well. He shared the dates and times that each neighbor was available.

Trey had been listening to Alex's half of the conversation and could tell by her reaction that she liked what she heard.

As soon as Alex hung up, she turned to him and shared the news about the upcoming interviews.

She asked him if he were up to a lunch treat on her.

After getting Trey's agreement to lunch she called Johnnie and invited him to lunch as well.

The rest of the afternoon was spent reviewing information about Annie's parents, friends, and neighbors with Trey. Alex engaged him as the devil's advocate. She wanted him to help eliminate useless questions. She wanted a razor-sharp focus for the interviews.

That evening as she thought about the next day, she decided to bake cookies. She made a batch of raison-oatmeal and a batch of chocolate chip cookies.

She made enough so she could share a few with Matt, who had been away on an EMT training event in Minneapolis and who she was looking forward to spending a quiet evening with on Friday.

She made enough for her office partners, the Chief, to take to Loveland and for Trey to take home to Nolan. She looked at the trays of cookies and laughed at her ambition. She knew it was driven by her anxiety and tension.

The cookies turned out to be a big hit at the office. Travis, who usually ribbed her, praised her instead for not only being able to shoot but also making great cookies. The Chief not only complimented her but told her that she had bought his approval for whatever she might next need. No asking necessary.

Trey thanked her for the cookies for Nolan and after having one of each with his morning coffee, he said Nolan would need to share the cookies.

This time Alex drove to Loveland, and it seemed to take twice as long as the previous trip.

She commented on the how long it was taking and attributed it to a reverse adrenaline rush. Trey laughed and said he had never heard of such a thing, but he would look into the theory.

She parked in the same spot as Trey had previously done. She noted that the parking lot was generously large, and she again wondered about its size.

She took her heaping plate of cookies and let Trey take the lead and open the doors.

The deputy behind the desk looked at her and smiled and said he was happy to see her. He flipped the switch and let them through the metal detector.

Alex handed him the plate of cookies and asked him to share it with everyone in the station. She kept several to take back to the Sheriff.

Alex greeted him as Sheriff Williams.

He reminded her that she had agreed to call him Evan.

Alex smiled and handed him the four cookies that she had brought for him and said that yes, she indeed had agreed to call him Evan.

The sheriff accepted the cookies and put them in the coffee pot area. He then poured three cups of coffee sat down and looked at them.

He remarked that he had not put so much time into a case for a long time. Studying the case and making notes had helped him get over how he felt after the interview a little over a week ago. He added that his wife had noticed the change and commented on its positive nature.

He had the neighborhood and childhood school friends of Anny all scheduled for interviews. Her parents were first and then on the schedule there was an interview with someone almost every afternoon or evening during the coming week, the weekend, and the following week. He asked if Alex and Trey had any issues or conflicts with the scheduled dates and times.

Alex looked at the schedule to be polite, but she knew that these interviews would be the focus of her attention, and she would accept any time of day or night. She looked at Trey to make sure he was OK. He was the one with a family.

He looked at her and said he was OK with the schedule but said that she and Matt would have to come over for lunch on Sunday and play with Nolan. Then he could go to the interview scheduled on that day.

Sheriff Evan, as Alex was now calling him smiled and said he recalled similar times when his partner would come over on Sunday for lunch and the two would go out on patrol together.

He looked at the clock in his office and commented that this time they would ride to the interview in an official police car.

Alex was quiet on the way to Annie's home. She had studied the case in such detail that she felt like she knew Annie's parents.

She was ready to run in and greet them like friends, but she knew that for them it was a personal and probably still a painful situation. She would listen carefully and try to reassure them that she was on the case because of her experience and that she was looking for any clue that might lead to solving the case.

The Sheriff led the way and rang the doorbell.

It was clear to Alex that he was well known to the Scots. They called him Evan. He got a hug from Annie's mother, Linda, and a handshake and man hug from her father, Stanley.

It was also clear to her that the sheriff had not told the Scots that she was Black. The reaction of the Scots was one that she always received. They were polite but noticeably surprised.

Linda led the way into the living room and asked if they would like a cup of coffee or water. She went on to say that she was getting coffee for herself. She commented that she would need it just to hold during the interview.

The sheriff set the tone and accepted a cup.

Alex had been looking at the family pictures and saw that at the center of the fireplace mantle was a picture of Annie standing between her parents.

She pulled her attention back to the moment and also accepted a cup of coffee.

Her keen attention to detail would play a critical role in her quest to solve the case. Her keen sensitivity to how people reacted would allow her to extract information that others had missed. Her own belief in her intuition allowed her to think the impossible and think beyond the limits others put on themselves.

She was determined to make a breakthrough in the case.

4 The Parents

Alex watched as Linda turned to walk to get the coffee. Alex immediately asked if she could help with the coffee. Linda paused for a moment and then smiled and replied that she would appreciate the help.

Once in the kitchen Linda stopped as she opened the cupboard where she had her cups. She looked at Alex and asked if she had any children.

Alex smiled and replied that she hoped to have some but so far, the right guy had not asked for her hand.

Linda replied that she hoped Alex would find the right guy.

She went on and told Alex that she had first turned down the sheriff's request for the interview. He had persisted and said that the best person possible was doing the investigation.

You have to understand how hard this is to relive Annie's disappearance.

I was surprised at the door.

He did not tell us you were Black.

He only said you were the best.

Alex again smiled and replied that her skin color usually presented a barrier and that over the years it made her motivated to succeed.

She went on to say that she planned to succeed in solving Annie's case. She repeated it in the affirmative saying that she would solve the case and that Linda would know Annie's fate in a few days or at the most a few weeks.

Linda looked at Alex. There were tears in her eyes as she replied that she hoped Alex was right.

Alex walked over and gave her a hug.

Linda thanked her and handed her one of the trays with cookies. She picked up the tray with the coffee, cream and sugar and led the way back to the living room.

Trey was sitting ramrod straight and stiff on the rocker. The sheriff had the large easy chair, and Stanley was sitting on the edge of a black recliner. All three seemed to be acting somewhat awkward.

The sheriff was telling a fishing story and surely exaggerating on the fact that his pole was bent, the line strength at its limit and the size of the fish was of record weight. Alex asked him if he had a picture of this fish, as she held the cookies in front of him.

She did not wait for a reply but went to Stanley and offered him some cookies. She then offered the cookies to Trey and quietly told him to sit back and relax. Afterwards she put the tray on the coffee table in front of where she planned to sit.

She sat down next to Linda, picked up her coffee and a cookie. She took a bite and a small sip of coffee. She had purposefully taken this action to let Linda get her composure. It was clear that the men were looking at her, expecting her to lead.

Alex put her hand on Linda's and apologized for resurfacing the pain of Annie's loss. She went on to explain that an unusual situation had caused her boss, the Cincinnati Chief of Police to want Annie's case to be re-examined. She made it clear that she and Trey had been assigned to resolve Annie's cold case. They had just finished a tough case and had expected a break. She finished by saying that both of them were committed to solving Annie's case.

She paused for a moment and then thanked Sheriff Evan for being such a strong supporter in getting Annie's case solved.

Alex then paused before asking her first question.

Who did they suspect when Annie first went missing? She threw out the possible suspect groups, a friend, a neighbor, a family member, a stranger.

Linda looked at her husband.

It was clear to Alex that Linda did suspect someone.

It was Stanley that replied that yes, they had two neighbors that they suspected. One was a single male neighbor who had purchased the house two houses away a year or so before Annie's disappearance. He was the only new neighbor and had moved in a few months before Annie went missing.

The other were the neighbors that lived across the street, but they had been there when Linda and he bought their home. He was a weird guy, and his wife was not very friendly. They never had any children. Linda had tried being neighborly, but it never worked out.

Linda continued that she was sure it had been one of the neighbors. She could not remember the last time a strange car had come into their cul-de-sac street. They had no local relatives, and she did not suspect any of them.

She went on to say that she felt guilt every day about not having accompanied Annie to her friend's house. She had always thought of the neighborhood as a safe area.

Alex squeezed Linda's hand and commented that she was not at fault. She went on to ask if there was anything else, she could remember.

Linda got up and went to a drawer of the desk that was across the hall in the sitting room turned into an office. She picked up a photo.

She brought the photo back into the living room and sat back down next to Alex.

She showed the picture to Alex.

She pointed to the clothes that Annie was wearing and explained that it was the outfit that Annie had on when she disappeared. She had been on the way to her friend's house to show off her new outfit.

It was the best picture that Alex had seen. It clearly showed a very beautiful, happy young girl. The red blouse and dark blue, almost black skirt made her look very mature or perhaps the word that came to Alex was stunning.

Alex carefully placed the picture on the table and took out her phone and took several snaps of the picture. She asked if Linda minded her taking a picture of the picture on the fireplace mantel. She took one of just the fireplace and the picture. Then she asked Linda and Stanley to stand on each side of the picture. Linda got up and took Stanley's hand and placed him on the same side he stood when the picture was taken.

Alex felt that if the story about a woman kept prisoner in the woods was true, the picture of Linda and Stanley with the picture of Annie might be useful later.

She looked over at Sheriff Evan and asked him if he had any questions. He shook his head to indicate that he had no questions. She looked at Trey and got the same negative nod.

She commented that she was done with the interview. Alex looked at Linda and thanked her for her hospitality and for once again enduring the emotional strain. She went on to let her know that she would get progress reports via the Sheriff and if there was any breakthrough she would personally call.

She then turned and walked slowly to the front door. She opened it for Trey and the Sheriff and then once again gave Linda a hug and quietly said that she was going to solve Annie's cold case.

The three of them walked out to the car and got in. The sheriff drove around the cul-de-sac and they all waved to Linda and Stanley who were standing outside their front door.

Alex thanked the Sheriff for having set up the meeting and asked how the interview had gone.

The Sheriff looked at her and replied that he was surprised at how smoothly Alex had conducted the meeting and how well she had connected with Linda. Linda had never shown him the picture of Annie or said anything about her going over to her friend to show off her new clothes. He went on to say that focusing on the picture on the mantel and getting both Linda and Stanley to get their picture taken with the mantel picture was unusual, but it seemed to please both of them.

He asked what Alex planned to do with the pictures.

Alex replied that if, and she stated the if with emphasis, she found Annie alive she felt that she would need proof that she was a person that knew Abbie's mother and father and could be trusted.

Alex went on and pointed out that if she were alive, Annie might be traumatized and very afraid.

The sheriff seemed surprised and asked if she really believed that Annie could still be alive?

Alex replied that when she had listened to Martha share her story and came to believe there was truth in it, she came to the realization that she had to also believe that Annie was alive. If the woman in the woods is her, she lives.

If it is some other poor woman then I will be wrong, but I will free that woman as part of my job.

The Sheriff looked at her and quietly added he hoped Alex was right about Annie. He commented that there were two interviews scheduled for the next day. The two happened to be the two households that Linda and Stanley had commented on in the interview.

He went on to comment that he had his personal bias and suspicion, but he would be mum until Alex had done her interviews.

Alex thanked him and said that she and Trey would be back the next day and go with him on the two interviews.

On the drive back to the station Alex noted that it was a quiet ride back to the station. She wondered if the interview had somehow affected Trey.

She decided that the best way to find out was to ask. She pulled off of the highway and headed toward Graeter's on Kenwood road. She liked the location because it was an easy off from I-71 and then an easy merge back going south.

Trey looked over to her as they got off 71 and asked what she had in mind.

She looked over at him and smiled and replied she either needed a drink of whisky or something sweet. Since they were both susceptible to the effects of alcohol, she figured Graeter's was the better choice.

As they walked in Trey said that he knew she was wondering what was going on.

Let's get our ice cream and then come back to the car and discuss it," Alex replied.

She did not like to have private discussions in public.

She looked at the choices and settled for a mango sorbet and was surprised when Trey chose the raspberry sorbet. She knew his favorite was the chocolate, chocolate chip.

She paid for both and on the way to the car she commented on his choice of raspberry sorbet.

Trey responded that it was the second time in a week that she had stopped for ice cream and he wanted to control the calories.

Once in the car Trey commented that he had gotten into the case in a personal way. He had imagined how he would have felt if Nolan was abducted. Even now he was worried about him. He admitted he had let the case become personal. He added that it was impossible not to.

Alex was quiet for a moment. Then she said that if she had a child, she too would be worried. They would both have to keep an eye on Nolan and make sure that when he was out in public or outside, he would be watched. She went on to say that she needed Trey to stay focused on Annie's case.

She suggested they go to Johnnie's place and see if he had gotten anywhere with his efforts.

She started the car and drove toward downtown. She realized that she had her own high level of anxiety about her ability to solve

Annie's case and her vision of what she might find frightened her and had become a dream or better said a nightmare that she had visited every night since she had read Johnnie's report.

She was glad that her AA meeting was the event of the evening. She and Trey would have a chance to air some of their anxiety.

The history of those abducted supported the anxiety that both she and Trey were experiencing. Alex had no clue that a hand from above found all things possible and in this case, it was leading her where she could not imagine.

It was leading her to a branch in life's path that she was unaware of.

<u>*5 Annie*</u>

It was early Monday. It was still dark. She was not completely sure of the date, but she was sure it was Monday. Jeff had left the evening before.

It was Monday!

She had a week to execute the escape she had planned for what seemed a lifetime.

Over the years she had patiently dug around the cement post that anchored her chain. She had used the extra cloth from sewing clothes to support a top layer of dirt so when Jeff inspected the post area it always appeared normal.

His checking always caused her heart to race. She knew if he found out he would put so much concrete into the hole that she would never be able to dig it up.

The girls had asked several times what she was doing. She told them it would be a special surprise, but they had to keep it secret.

Tears flowed freely as she struggled to pull up the cement post that held the bolt to which her ankle chain was tethered. She pulled it out onto the floor. It had been a Herculean effort on her part. She had no way to smash it or to get her chain loose.

She was prepared.

She had the girl's wagon with which she would pull the anchor and chain and her two daughters. It was a big wagon that Jeff had brought to the cabin just recently. He had decided that the girls would go with them on the walk through the woods that he always took her on. It was the only time she was free from the ankle chain.

She was determined to make her escape. She wanted her daughters to have a normal life. Her daughters needed to see, understand, and appreciate the wonders that were beyond the forest and valleys.

It was her duty to free them.

She recalled the day her new neighbor, Jeff, abductor, and the father of her two daughters had drugged her and brought her to this cabin. It seemed a lifetime ago. She had kept track of the days, and it was the fifteenth year.

He had chained her after her first attempted to escape. He had caught her and tied her to a chair. He had disappeared and a long time later returned with a chain, a steel ring for her ankle, and the cement and foot long bolt with a ring at the top. The chain and bolt were joined and welded.

The chain was long and heavy. It was long enough for her to go out on the cabin porch to a hanging swing bench and to each end of the porch.

Jeff supplied all her needs. He brought her books to read. She did not want to be dumb and asked for history books, the classics, math, and science books. When she asked for magazines and a newspaper, Jeff had said no. When she asked for painting supplies, he had given her books on painting and an extensive supply of various paints.

It was clear to her that in his mind he was a kind, good guy. He wanted her to like him and later he expressed his love for her.

Reading and painting became her passion. She dreaded Jeff's coming but for the first few years he just engaged in talking to her and taking her on walks in the woods.

She liked the walks and gathered various objects that she later used as models that she incorporated into her drawings. She placed these objects around the edge of the cabin porch. It was a collection of rocks, bones, wooden limbs and even the skull of what she thought might be a bear.

When she had her first period Jeff had informed her that she was now a woman and no longer a girl. She had not been sure how to act but the routine of going for a walk and just talking continued for another two years. Then it changed.

He replaced the twin bed in her room with a new queen sized one. That night he gave her some sheer lingerie and asked her to put it on for him.

This was the turning point of their relationship. She was thoroughly embarrassed, humiliated, and terrified all at the same time. It was the first time she experienced sex. He was gentle and he was constantly telling her how much he loved her.

She did not reply and was sure she was more of a log than a person. She cried the rest of the night and was thankful when he left the next day. She stood under the shower for hours and continued to cry.

She painted the scene of her mind in black, grey and red. It was an abstract that no one but she would know its meaning. It was a painting of the horror that was instilled in her.

Jeff's subsequent visits included walks in the woods, but sex always occurred at night. She grew tired of hearing how they would have a lovely family. The chain on her ankle was a constant reminder that she had not agreed to this relationship. It was abhorrent.

Being secluded and alone was frustrating. She knew the world was marching on and she remained ignorant of what was happening. She tried to imagine what her school friends were doing and if they were going to go to college. She knew that her mother and father had constantly described going to college as her future.

Their encouragement had driven her to set up a study routine at home. As a captive her mother's voice still guided her. She read all the classics; she progressed through math finding it easy and intriguing. She loved history.

The books on Art history and the various artists were her favorites. She knew better than to try to copy any of their styles, but she learned their techniques and she crafted her own style and vision.

She wondered how her parents were doing. She wondered if she had any younger brothers or sisters. Not knowing created a void in her mind. She hoped that her parents had moved on with their lives. She was sure they thought of her as dead.

She had named her first daughter after her mother. The second after one of her favorite aunts who she thought of as exotic. Their arrival had saved her from losing herself in her introspection and feeling of depravation. They were her gems of hope.

Linda now six interrupted her thoughts and asked what she was doing. She had just finished pulling the cement post out of the ground.

She knelt and hugged Linda and pulled Lorie now five to her. She looked at each of them and told them that they were going for a walk in the woods.

Putting the post up onto the wagon turned out to be a bigger challenge than she had anticipated. She took the removeable sides of the wagon off on the ends and one side. She placed the wagon against the base of the porch and tried to lift the post onto the wagon. She could not risk trying to roll it into the wagon. If it fell on the ground, she would never be able to pick it up.

She tried again to lift the post and realized she would never be able to lift it into the wagon. She sat down on the wagon and cried.

She thought about using a lever system, but she had no lever that would be strong enough. Then she thought about a pulley arrangement. She looked toward the door where Jeff had put a chin up bar. She moved the wagon into the doorway and centered the wagon under the bar. She pulled her chain over the bar.

The chain moved easily over the pipe, and she was able to lift the cement post. It took all her strength and some imaginative body and hip movement to get the anchor onto the wagon. She realized that once she got the wagon moving, she would need to be careful not to tip it over.

She moved the anchor to the front of the wagon and used some heavy cord to tie it securely in place. She covered it with a small comforter so that it would not scratch the girls. She carefully moved the wagon out, and off, the porch. She had piled up her collection of objects and put a layer of soil over them to create a crude ramp.

Then she put the girls in.

She had a heavy comforter, a large piece of heavy-duty plastic and a few canned good in the wagon. The extra clothes for the girls and herself were used as padding around the girls.

She then shouldered her backpack loaded with food and began her journey into what she hoped would be her escape and freedom.

She chose not to go down the road because she remembered that there were no homes for what seemed an eternity. She did not want to be caught out in the open. She hoped for a safe haven by the time Jeff returned.

A few hours later she realized that she was lost. She was not sure if she was walking in circles or just going in the wrong direction. When she came to where small flow of water was running down a small groove in the side of a steep bank, she decided it was time to feed the girls and make camp for the night.

She planned to follow the water. She hoped it would flow ever larger streams and maybe a river and people.

It took her about an hour to erect a makeshift tent with the plastic. She had placed the plastic in such a manner that it served as the floor and folded over and served as the top as well. She suspended her chain across two poles to hold up the top of the plastic and used her supply of pieces of twine to tie it off.

The comforter was large enough for the three of them to lay on and then fold over them.

She made a point of letting the girls know that this was a camping adventure, and they should have fun. They each roasted a hot dog over the fire and shared a tin cup to drink the water from the stream.

She knew that no matter what, this was one positive moment that she would remember. She told the girls stories and took out her sketch book and did renderings of the two as they held their hot dogs over the small fire that she had made.

The night sky was filled with countless stars. She pointed out the big dipper to Linda and Lorie. She went on to tell stories about the ancient gods and how they had ruled the earth. She succumbed to telling the story of the three bears when her daughters said they would rather hear it.

The girls were soon sleeping. She had her arms around each of them and managed to fold the comforter over them and herself. She lay there for a long time gazing at the stars, enjoying the warmth of her daughters, and praying that she could make her escape.

It took her most of the following morning to get everything ready to move on.

She had decided that following the small stream would be the best action to take. It should lead to ever larger streams and eventually to people. To people rattled loosely in her mind.

Having to pull the wagon made going slow and she often had to take round about ways to follow the stream.

When the sun was high in the sky she stopped for lunch. This time she did not light a fire but chose to feed the girls a salami sandwich. The bread had gotten compressed in the backpack and they all laughed at eating a sandwich with flat multigrain bread. "Ugly but good for you," they chanted in unison.

Linda said they should go camping more often.

Annie replied that they would go as often as they could, and they would go all over the country and enjoy its beauty.

At the moment, her mind was on her escaped. She knew that in four days Jeff would arrive at the cabin and find her missing. She had tried to erase her trail, but the wagon trail was hard to hide. She was sure if she did not make it into some town or find someone's home Jeff would have no trouble tracking her down.

She was not sure what would happen. She was sure he would not hurt the girls, but she was certain that her life would be in peril.

The small stream had merged with a larger stream that gurgled and ran over countless polished rock rapids. This was a good sign but now the banks along the stream were steeper and it was hard to keep the wagon from turning over.

She had the girls walk behind her so she could better handle the wagon and its load of the anchor and excess chain. Walking with the chain around her ankle had been a challenge and on the steeper slope keeping the wagon up right also became a challenge.

In several places she had to stand on the downhill side and move sideways so she could hold the wagon upright.

She found a sturdy stick that fit through the ring of the chain and kept the excess chain from coming out of the wagon as she walked. It was still slow going but it seemed to be at the speed that the two girls could easily keep up with.

They were having fun running ahead or to the sides to see what they could find.

Once again, she looked for a place to set up camp as the gurgling stream ran into yet a larger one. The new stream was about ten feet across and ran a little slower. The surrounding area also promised a flatter area on which to travel.

She found a large fallen tree. She was going to make her camp in the root basin created when the tree fell over but decided against it when she saw what looked like rain clouds moving in overhead. She instead chose a spot where the fallen tree branched and where there was a downward slope toward the stream. The plastic was large enough to wrap over the top of the tree branches and around to the stream side to provide a floor. She placed some of the larger broken tree limbs to hold the plastic on top, a long slender branch to make the back fold along the ground and used stones to hold the sides of the bottom. The comforter would again serve as the sleeping bag.

Dinner was again a fun affair. She had carried some dry mac and cheese in single serve packages. She heated some of the stream water in her stainless-steel mug and poured into the mac and cheese mix. While getting the mac and cheese ready she kept the girls busy by having them give each other a wet washcloth bath.

The giggling and excited chattering warmed her heart. She loved her daughters, and her escape was as much for them as it was for herself.

She promised herself that she would make her escape.

This was the end of day two. The sky turned black, and the thunder brought fear to the surface. The first bolt of lightning caused them to get under their makeshift tent and huddle together with the comforter to hide in.

Annie did not feel totally safe. When the rain began falling, she pulled the floor plastic over them as far as possible and positioned the rocks to hold the plastic in pace.

The rain that followed was more than Annie had ever experience. It seemed they were located under a flowing waterfall.

She was proud of the fact that the cover she had made was keeping them dry. She held her daughters and told them some of their favorite stories.

They soon fell asleep. Annie soon followed when the storm intensity reduced to a steady but not too heavy rain.

Annie awoke to the noise of rain on the plastic above her. She looked out and could see that it would likely rain the whole day.

This was of concern to her, but she was not going to chance leading the girls through the rain and getting sick.

The eggs she had carried seemed to the perfect choice for breakfast. She told the girls to sit under the shelter and read the storybook she gave them.

She took most of her out clothes off and went out to boil eggs. Getting a fire started proved to be impossible. She changed the morning menu to salami sandwich made with smashed bread.

She dried off and gave the girls their breakfast.

Once again, they all laughed about the smashed bread, but they all enjoyed it.

After getting dressed she leaned against the tree limb behind her and took out her sketchbook. She spent the grey wet morning making sketches of the girls and the scene of the stream and forest beyond.

She wished that the chain around her ankle was gone and that she was truly free.

Annie's tenacity, determination and drive were providing the time needed for the hand from above to guide the help the help that was trying to find her. Her ability to maintain her sanity under such bizarre conditions was the basis that would eventually lead to her freedom.

6 Explosive Verification

Sleep had not come easy. Alex knew she was into the case too deep, but she could not get her mind off of Annie. She went to the gym and put in another three-mile jog. The clock by her bed had a large twelve when she pulled her comforter over her. She knew she would be tired the next day. She had two interviews one early in the afternoon and one at six.

After a quick breakfast of soft boiled eggs and a piece of toast she pushed her bike into the elevator. Her bike ride to the station gave her the chance to wake up and decide what she wanted to do while she and Trevor waited until their interviews in Annie's neighborhood.

Johnnie came into the coffee area as she was looking at the donuts someone had placed by the coffee pot. After saying good morning, he complained that she could have given him a ride so that he would not have had to walk.

He had no qualms at selecting an apple fritter and leading the way to her desk. He took a chair at Trevor's desk.

He took a bite of his fritter and a sip of his coffee. He went on to say that he planned to use the police data base to see if he could find any additional information about the two neighbors that Alex would be interviewing. He apologized about having come up cold in his other searches.

Alex took a sip of her black coffee and wished that she had weakened and taken the bear claw she had eyed in the coffee area. She looked at Johnnie and with a small chuckle mentioned that it was called a cold case for a reason.

Trey walked in with a cup of black coffee in one hand and a bear claw sweet roll in the other.

Alex greeted him and told him that he would have to give her a bite of the bear claw. She watched as he smiled waved the sweet in the air and teased her that it was all his. He then sat down and handed her half of it.

Alex thanked him and praised him as the best partner she ever worked with.

Yeah! I'm the only one willing to work with you, everyone else asked for body armor and when they were rejected, they all declined. He joked.

Johnnie had identified Annie's grade school friends and given the list to Alex.

Alex spent the morning putting in calls to them and had discussions with each of them. Annie had been very well liked and one young man mentioned that he still missed her to this very day and thought of her often.

He wished Alex luck in closing the case. He asked that she let him know when she did so he could move on with his life.

After having spent the morning making these calls and watching Trey studying the notes that Johnnie had sent them, she asked what he had in mind for lunch.

She was surprised when Trevor at the next desk commented that he would like to take in the new restaurant in Mariemont and see whether it was as good as he had heard.

Alex smiled and said that it sounded like a good place to try, and it was on the way to Loveland.

During lunch Bill, Trevor's partner and the more polite and conventional one of the two, asked how her investigation into the cold case was progressing.

Alex answered that her apartment had gotten more cleaning in one week than the entire month before. She admitted that Annie's cold case was a tension builder. The more she and Trey dug in the more it affected them personally.

She shared the interview with Annie's parents and the impact that the interview had on the two of them. She went on to say that it had a pint of ice cream and a six-mile run impact on her. Trey added that for him it was the pint of ice cream and the whole night spoiling his son. He confessed that he had not been so impacted since his Iraqi combat.

Travis shared the discussion he had with Sheriff Williams. He said he had told the sheriff that if the cold case was going to be solved she would do it.

Alex thanked Travis for his support and then teasingly told him that the sheriff thought Travis was getting soft because he had been so supportive of her. She and Travis were always trading back handed compliments. It was friendly and it kept the group from getting too serious.

It had been a long lunch, but it was still too early for the interviews.

Alex decided that she and Trey would go shopping. She wanted to stop using bottled water and had seen that Costgood had a pitcher that had a carbon filter. This would let her eliminate the cases of bottled water that she used each week. She figured her carbon footprint was the size of a sasquatch's footprint.

Trey laughed when she shared the image with him. He called Lindsey and asked if she wanted anything from Costgood. He vocally listed her order of milk, eggs, multigrain bread, and a rotisserie chicken. Oh! And a bottle of wine he continued.

Trey filled his order, but Alex realized that the sale for the pitcher was a week away and she decided that her water would run out at the same time that the pitcher was on sale.

She received a call from Sheriff Williams. He apologized and said that it was his wife's birthday, and he had promised to take her to a movie and dinner. He would not be able to be part of the interviews of the two neighbors. He asked if Alex wanted to reschedule the interviews.

Alex replied that she would do the interviews and update him the next day and that he should make his wife's birthday special and buy desert on her.

There was no way she would delay the interviews. She told the sheriff to wish his wife happy birthday. She turned to Trey and asked if he were OK to do the interviews on their own.

He laughed and replied that at the last interview, the sheriff and he were just there to make it look official and she did all the talking.

They arrived and parked the car at the top of the cul-de-sac loop and walked back to the house across the street from the Scots.

It was quickly clear during the interview that the across the street neighbors might be strange and not very friendly, but they shared that if they ever had a child, they would have wanted one as polite and friendly as Annie. They recalled the day Annie brought them a plate of warm oatmeal-raisin cookies that she had baked. They hoped that Annie's case could be solved.

Alex thanked them for their time and agreed to let them know when the case was solved.

It was time for the next interview. The house they walked toward was one that was at the top of the cul-de-sac circle where they had parked the car. It was a brick two story with a front porch the width of the section that came forward toward the street. The yard was well kept and the house in good shape.

It was clear that the neighborhood had all been built at about the same time and probably by the same builder. The styles were all similar and only windows; doors and the color of bricks and paint differed.

Alex wasn't sure but she thought she saw someone looking out the upstairs window. She mentioned it to Trey who verified that he had seen the same thing.

Alex rang the doorbell. There was a moment of waiting but then the door opened.

She and Trey showed their badges and introduced themselves. The person at the door introduced himself as Jeff Thomas and asked them to come in. He said that he thought the sheriff would be part of the interview.

Alex explained the sheriff's wife birthday as she sat down.

The interview went smoothly, and nothing surfaced that would make Alex think that he had anything to do with Annie's disappearance.

She walked out of the house with a feeling of disappointment. She had hoped that one of the two interviews would give her a lead.

She took out the car keys and was playing with the remote start feature as she and Trey walked silently toward it.

On her first attempt the windows went down. She and Trey stopped as she looked at the fob and found the correct button to push.

She pressed the button to start the car.

The area in front of her became a fireball as an explosion lifted the car at least twenty feet into the air. She felt herself lifted by a powerful blast of air and seemed to float back through the air as if she was flying backward.

She remembered her Tae Kwon Do instructor teaching her class how to fall and instinctively slammed her hand down as she landed. Even so she knew she would have a bruised butt.

She could not hear a thing and had blood dripping from her fingers, but she turned and immediately ran back toward the house that they had just left.

She opened the door and was just about to step in when a hand on her shoulder pulled her back.

It was Trey and he was pointing down at a thin wire. "Trap," he mouthed as he pointed to each side of the house. "Careful," he mouthed again as he went toward the side.

They both came around the house to the back and went to the garage at the back. The car was still there. They turned to the house and went carefully up to the back door. It was ajar and there was another trip wire.

Alex put in a call to the sheriff. She could barely hear him. She was shouting at her phone when she realized that explosion had affected her hearing. Now she understood why Trey had mouthed the words. His battle experience had come through. She had a new level of respect for him. His past experience in house-to-house fighting had saved her life.

It was clear that someone had already called the sheriff. He told her that his people were seconds away and he would be there in a few minutes.

Alex stayed in back and Trey went to the front. He had indicated with hand gestures that he thought there was no one inside.

Alex thought about what she wanted to do. She was now sure that Jeff Nolan, who had passed his interview with flying colors, was indeed the person who had abducted Annie. She vowed to hunt him down.

Even though she could barely hear, she put in a call to Johnnie. She asked him to check every person that had ever known Jeff Nolan or had spoken to him or been distantly related to him. She basically begged Johnnie to give her a lead.

Johnnie replied that he would work on it but that she should stop shouting.

A thought came to her, and she asked Johnnie to check all land records for the counties in the Finger Lake area and the counties in northern Pennsylvania. He should look for a transfer of property near the time of Annie's abduction. She wanted to know the names of anyone doing the transfers.

She let him know that she was going to be at his apartment door in the next hour and went on to say that, if in the future he wanted any additional free lunches he better find a lead.

She called the Chief and told him the situation and that she needed a car. She shared that she planned to immediately start driving toward the Finger Lake area.

The Chief reacted in the same way Johnnie had and told her she would get what she wanted without the need to shout.

One of the sheriff's deputies came around the side of the house and told her that the EMT's were out front and wanted to check her out.

Alex accepted the care given by the EMT team. They removed some glass shards from her arm and wanted to take her to the hospital for additional observation and test.

Alex thanked them but declined a trip to the hospital.

She knew she needed to move fast. The guilty person was on the run and if Annie was in the forest around the finger lakes her life was now on the line.

This reminded her that she had not talked to Mathew with whom she had a dinner date planned.

She made the call explained the situation, assured him that she was alright and that his brethren EMT's in Loveland had patched her up.

He gave chuckle and commented that her hearing would return, and he was pleased to hear her shouting at him.

Her hearing had come back to about fifty percent. She looked at Trey and asked if he was willing to start driving toward the Finger Lake region.

He nodded in the affirmative. He then called home and let Lindsey know.

The sheriff had arrived and had taken stock of the situation. Once he was sure everyone was alright, he asked what Alex needed.

She replied that she needed a ride down to her office and she wished she could have a slug of whisky.

He said OK to the ride, but she would have to supply her own whisky.

There was no way for Alex to know that her determination would be the key element that would make the ultimate difference to in the lives of every person involved. Single handedly she was taking the steps that would be a positive element that would affect her the rest of her life.

The pain from her wounds and bruises failed to register as she concentrated on getting to Jeff before he could take whatever action he might be planning.

Her fear was that he had demonstrated that he would take drastic action to protect his perverted world.

7 The Cabin

lex was anxious to get going. She felt that they had to somehow overtake Jeff before he reached wherever he was going. He had abandoned his house and his car. She wondered whether he owned a motorcycle or was using a car from the shop where he worked as a mechanic.

It did not escape her that he had tried to kill them both and that had made it a very personal matter. He was now dead center as her target.

Sheriff Williams asked if it was alright with Alex if he came in with her and met her boss. Alex was still recovering from the force and sound of the explosion. She pointed to her ears and mouthed, "I can't hear you." Then she smiled and said that it would be great if he met with her boss and gave him the keys to her now non-existent car.

The sheriff took the keys and said he would do it if she promised to call him Evan.

Alex replied that if Evan could get her another new car, she would take he and his wife out to dinner to make up for having interrupted his wife's birthday celebration.

He smiled and said it was a deal.

The three of them were met by the Chief as they passed the entrance security area. He took in the bandage on her left arm and asked if she was alright.

Alex replied that her butt was hurting more than her arm. She introduced Evan, Sheriff of Loveland. "I am to call him Evan but until you earn the right, you have to call him Sheriff Williams," she went on.

She watched as the two shook hands and then Evan held out the keys to her car to her boss. "Here are the keys to Alex's car, they saved her life. She needs another set to another new car," he said politely handing the keys over.

The Chief laughed and took the keys. He looked at her and said that he had promised to get her anything she wanted when he had eaten her cookies. He went on to say that he was reneging on the promise and needed another tray of cookies before he would keep it.

They all walked into the Chief's office where he proceeded to offer coffee and donuts.

Alex declined the coffee. She suggested that the Chief and Evan discuss the situation. She planned to leave immediately and head for the Finger Lakes region.

The Chief handed her the keys to their new rescue and prisoner transport van. It was the same one that she and Trey had driven to Mississippi just about two months ago. He asked her not to get it blown up and also to bring it back with no bullet holes.

Alex thanked him and let him know that she and Trey were going toward the Alleghany National Forest, Finger Lakes area. She would let everyone know exactly where when she knew the location.

The Chief wished her good luck in her hunt and told Trey to keep them both safe.

Alex and Trey left immediately for her apartment.

They were met by Lindsey, who had brought a travel bag of personal clothes and other necessary items for Trey.

Mathew was waiting as well. He did a quick inspection of the bandage on her arm. He joked with her that she didn't have to think up such an elaborate scheme to get out of their date that evening. Then he again volunteered to come along.

Johnnie was beside himself. He fidgeted and pranced around the group holding a thick tan copy paper sized envelope.

It was clear to Alex that he was anxious to tell her something.

She hushed everyone, pointed to Johnnie, and asked if he knew the route she would be driving.

Johnnie held up his arms, did a twirl, and kept saying yes, yes, yes. He went on to say that her idea to check county records in Pennsylvania and counties around the Finger Lakes of New York was the breakthrough. He had found the record that transferred property in the Mohannon State Forest area of Pennsylvania to one Jeff Nolan Thomas.

He went on to show several maps he had printed out that led to a cabin in the forest near the park. The cabin was miles into a deeply forested area.

Alex had tears welling in her eyes as she gave him a hug and then loudly called him a search genius.

Everyone crowded onto the elevator. The elevator up to the sixth floor seemed to take forever. She walked quickly down the hallway with everyone following.

She opened the door and went straight to her closet and retrieved the cooler on wheels that she had used only once before. She opened her freezer and retrieve frozen hot dogs, ice cream, and hamburger meat. Next, she opened the fridge portion and took out all the vegetables.

She went into the bedroom and quickly packed her bag.

She came out and declared it was time to go.

Once again, she was in the lead. She went out the front doors to the large black square police transport van parked on the street with its lights flashing.

The large gold lettering Cincinnati Police Transport on the shiny black paint made the square bodied van a formidable site.

Alex tossed the keys to Trey and got in on the passenger side. She entered the address of the Youngstown police station into the van's GPS as Trey drove toward the North I-71 entrance ramp.

When she opened the folder Johnnie had given her, she realized the sun was on its way down. She turned on the overhead spotlight so she could study the maps and information Johnnie had organized.

Johnnie had marked Brookville Pennsylvania as the last location on a major highway. Alex did some quick calculations to see if there was a way to make up for the time that it had taken for Trey and her to get on the road. Jeff had left his home immediately before the explosion. She and Trey were several hours behind. There was no way to recapture the time lost but she wanted to get as much of it back as possible.

Her calculations indicated that eight-five miles per hour was the speed that made the most sense to her. She flipped on the vans red flashing lights and told Trey the speed to set on the cruise control.

He smiled at her and commented that he had always wanted to drive like a mad man.

The drive was as fast as made sense, but it was still tedious. They stopped only for brief moments either at rest stops or gas stations.

Lindsey had packet them several sandwiches and a variety of fruit snacks. She and Trey took turns passing out the food and snacks.

At the speed they were traveling, Alex made sure they switched every thirty minutes. She did not want to create an accident.

They made Brooksville at ten thirty at night. Alex shared the fact that she believed Annie was still alive, but events now made her fear that Jeff might now kill her and dispose of her body. She asked Trey what he thought.

Trey looked at her and replied that if she was right about Annie still being alive then he was sure Jeff would most likely kill her and hide her body as soon as he could.

Alex looked at Trey and suggested they fill up on gas and see if they could find the cabin during the night. She felt that if they could find the cabin before morning it would give Annie the best chance to survive.

She made a small prayer that Jeff had stopped somewhere for the night.

Johnnie had carefully marked the map through the forest to the cabin. The dark of night made following it challenging.

Trey was driving and Alex concentrated on where they were on the map.

She desperately wanted to get to the cabin first.

Trey drove at ten to fifteen miles per hour along a narrow road through dense forest. He made the comment that they had gone from one speed extreme to the opposite one.

Alex agreed. And said she wanted to step on his foot and blast ahead.

Then the cabin loomed out from the dark into the headlights.

Trey cut the headlights and stopped the van about a hundred yards from the cabin.

No lights came on in the cabin. Alex slid open the door on her side. The night was quiet except for the normal noises of the forest.

It seemed eerily quiet and ominous.

She instinctively pulled her gun from its shoulder holster. Trey slid his door open, and they both got out.

They carefully approached the cabin. All was silent. There was no car visible.

Trey tapped Alex on the shoulder. In the dark he indicated that he would go around back. She should stay out front. He would verbally announce their arrival and then she was to repeat it.

They both continued going toward the cabin.

Trey went around back.

Alex waited to hear his announcing that the Police had the cabin surrounded and those inside should proceed out the front door.

Alex then proceeded to repeat what Trey had said.

After a few moments. Trey repeated the command.

No lights had come on. There was no response.

Alex then announced at the top of her voice that the police were coming in.

The door was not locked, and Alex was quickly inside and had swept the room with her small handheld flashlight. Trey came in through the back and did the same. They methodically went through the rooms of the cabin.

It was empty. But it was clear that more than one person lived in it. The cabin had four rooms. Three bedrooms were at the front half of the cabin and the other half was one large area with the kitchen on one end. It had windows all around and a large covered back porch.

Trey went out to bring the van to the cabin. He drove the van behind the house.

Meanwhile Alex continued her inspection of the cabin. There were electrical lights but there was no electricity. Trey commented that there was a shed near the van that had an electric generator in it. He also commented that there was an outhouse as well.

Alex carefully examined each room. What she found surprised her. The clothes, books, a huge stack of very well-done paintings clearly indicated that three people lived in the house. From the clothes Alex found she surmised that it was Annie and two young girls.

It became clear to her that someone had been anchored to a central point. There was a deep hole about a foot in diameter at the center of the cabin. She was sure it had been an anchor point. The wooden floor around this point was scratched where a chain or other restraint had been repeatedly dragged.

She found a photo of the two young girls with the woman that she was certain could only be an older Annie.

Alex had a surge of relief that Annie was still alive and must have made her escape. Alex felt a surge of anxiety as she wondered where Jeff might be. She wondered if he had arrived ahead of them.

She shared her findings with Trey. She showed him the deep hole in the center of the cabin and the markings on the floor and said that it appeared Annie had probably been restrained by a chain. She had been a captive for all these years.

She was sure they had found where Annie had lived for many years. The question now standing before Alex like a fire breathing dragon was she too late to save her?

Had she caused Annie's death?

She led the way to the front of the cabin and examined the dirt road for several hundred yard back along the way they had come. The only fresh tire tracks were those of the van they had driven.

She felt relieved to have arrived ahead of Jeff. Now they had to find Annie.

Trey led the way back around to the back of the cabin. He found the faint trail of a wagon that seemed heavily loaded. Annie had tried to erase the tracks but even in the dark any good tracker would easily follow the trail.

He commented that he would be able to track where Annie had gone.

Alex replied that they should put on their back packs and go find Annie. She wanted to find Annie and get her to safety before Jeff could cause her any harm.

At the last moment she stopped and went to the van. She handed Trey his light Kevlar vest and she put on her own.

Together, in the pitch darkness of a moonless night they slowly followed what to Trey was a clear trail.

Alex was again impressed with another skill he had that she had not known about.

He had activated Alex's phone compass and had instructed her to log the steps of the pedometer and the heading into the notes App.

The going was slow until they got to the first camp and then Trey noted that Annie had chosen to follow the small stream. This made the going somewhat easier and much faster. They soon found the second and third camps.

The compass indicated an almost perfect U shape turn that seemed about a mile wide. Annie was following the flow of the water, but the water would take her back almost to where she had started. She would be very close to the cabin as she made her way.

The sun was rising when they found the fourth camp. It was located where the small creek met a larger almost river sized stream. Annie was almost to the main road which led up to the cabin!

Trey commented that they had crossed a small bridge on the way up to the cabin. Unknowingly Annie had closed the U and made it into a tear drop.

Alex wanted to scream out, "No!"

The sun was just breaking over the eastern ridge of mountains when Trey pointed ahead where a small fire was flickering a long distance ahead.

This seemed to be a signal to Alex. She dropped her backpack and took off at a sprint. She was now worried about the proximity of Annie and the two children to the bridge of the road that led to the cabin. They would be sitting ducks if Jeff saw them when he arrived.

Her conditioning would pay a dividend that Alex would forever cherish. Her feet barely touched the ground. If someone were to have timed her run, they would have found they had recorded the fastest mile on record. She was not running for her life she was running for the three lives she knew were sitting in sight of the bridge.

She was not to be denied. The pain that cursed through her body went unnoticed. She had her mind focused on speed. At the moment it had no other purpose.

8 Jeff

Pit Face Nolan" as he still thought of himself even after all the years since high school, drove north on I-71 toward his destination of Akron. He was staying five miles an hour below the speed limit. He was driving a car he had "borrowed" from the mechanic shop at which he worked. He planned to change vehicles by Monday morning when the borrowing became known.

He had watched the explosion from the second story window. The strength of the blast surprised him and when the blast blew in the upstairs window, he was glad that he had been hiding to the side behind the curtains.

He had learned to make the bomb online and where to buy the materials, but he had no idea about the strength that the quantity of the C4 would hold.

He could not believe that both of the detectives had survived the blast, but he saw that they were recovering.

He ran downstairs, set the front and back trip wires that he hoped would either delay of kill anyone coming after him and then ran out the back door. He took the neighbors bike and rode it to the garage where he had access to a car.

He cursed as he realized that his attempt to kill the two detectives had failed.

He had hoped to eliminate them and the Loveland Sheriff as well. For years he had feared the actions of the Sheriff, but he had been a no show for the interview.

As he thought about the situation, he was now in, he figured the idea of blowing up the car had been a miscalculation.

Water under the bridge he concluded.

He now had to get to the cabin and clean up the situation there. Then disappear. He had to figure out exactly what he had to do.

His experience at Sandy Point High of being mocked, being excluded from the school's social activities and being "Pit Face" made his graduation feel like a release from prison. He celebrated his graduation alone out in the forest that he loved.

He went to work as a mechanic. His first job was at a shop where he received excellent training.

He lived with his parents and dutifully saved his money. Other than bowling and going to the movies, there was little to do.

He did without a car and borrowed the old one to go out to go hiking in the forest.

Highly trained, but the slow and careless in the way he did his work led to his being fired. He went rapidly through several other local mechanic jobs. Each time he either left because he did not get along with his boss or he was fired for a similar reason.

His last boss held out the new oil rod seals that he had chosen not to install on the valves. He was told he was through and that the other shops had been notified about Jeff's incompetence.

There would not be another job for him in the region.

Jeff felt he was being singled out. He fantasized beating up or killing his boss but knew that he would only fantasize.

He decided he should leave the state and go and restart his life. He was a Cincinnati Reds baseball fan. They were his favorite team. They were the little underdog team that seemed to outperform the biggies. He figured Cincinnati would be a good place for him. He ordered the Cincinnati Inquirer and began looking for a job.

A few weeks later, he landed one in the Landen area. He found a convenient apartment nearby at a price he could afford.

He bade his parents goodbye and got on the bus. His possessions fit in two old suitcases given to him by his parents. He went across the country by bus and arrived at his destination three days later.

He made the long walk to work for several weeks while he saved his money. He finally was able to buy a fifteen-year-old car that was brought in for service.

After several months he had established a routine of working hard throughout the week. Bowling on Thursday night, having a few beers at a sports bar on Friday nights and then going to some state park to hike on the weekend.

He felt great about turning his life around.

He had been working for a few months when he was contacted by a lawyer that represented his great aunt, Anastasia. She had been the one person that he had always gotten along with and who had taken him on several camping trips when he was a kid. She had become a recluse. She never married and lived by herself in the forest. She left everything to him. He inherited her cabin in the woods. He initially thought about moving into the cabin but realized that he was not a hermit. He enjoyed his bowling, a Thursday or Friday night at the sports bar and he need to work for an income.

He liked his work.

He had changed his attitude at work and concentrated on making his customers happy. They came in and asked for him. He made a point of getting along with his boss.

He took the money that his great aunt had left him and found a home in the Loveland area.

He thought that his life was now on an upward trajectory.

A few days after he moved in the doorbell, which sounded like a clock chime went off.

He opened the door and looked into eyes that immediately made him fall in love. Standing before him was the most beautiful person he had ever encountered. She held out a plate of oatmeal and chocolate chip cookies and welcomed him to the neighborhood and after he thanked her, she turned and left. He knew then that she was the one.

She was the one, but she was so young.

Each passing day after that his feelings for her grew. He controlled himself for more than a year and finally he was overwhelmed with the desire for her.

He watched her coming and going carefully. He noted the times she went passed his house and then between the houses next door to a house on the next street. He packed his car and waited for the right moment. The moment arrived on a Friday afternoon right after he had returned from work. He immediately put some chloroform on a cotton swab and walked out as she approached his house.

She was dressed in a beautiful outfit as if she had dressed for him.

He had no desire to hurt her. He approached her from behind and put the cloth with chloroform over her nose and mouth. He carefully took her through the house and to his car. He gently laid her across the back seat.

He then went into the house and made sure all the lights were off and the house ready for the weekend. He then drove slowly out and went north toward Columbus on his way to the cabin.

The trip to the cabin was uneventful.

But the next day Annie tried to escape. He easily tracked her down and brought her back to the cabin.

He had planned to bring her to the cabin, but he had not thought through the details on how he would keep her there. When he brought her back from her escape attempt, he knew that somehow, he had to restrain her and keep her from leaving. It was then he decided how he would handle the situation.

It came to him. He would chain her.

He tied her to a chair and left to get the things he needed.

He went back to Youngstown and randomly selected a hardware store where he purchased cement, a long hardened stainless chain, a long bolt with a ring. He stopped by an auto repair shop and asked them to put the chain into the ring and then weld the ring shut. He had them do the same with a larger flat band. He had selected a band that would fit an ankle. When asked about the chain he said he raised horses and was trying out a way to tether them. He paid cash for all his transactions.

He chained Annie up.

He made sure the chain gave her access to every part of the cabin. He made sure she had food and showed her how to prime the sink hand pump to get water. He made sure she could get to all the necessities. He also taught her how to run he electric generator but warned her that she could only run it for a couple of hours a day.

Annie was not very nice or polite in her protest and called him every despicable thing she could possibly have called him, but he knew that over time she would come to like him. He planned to be kind.

When he was sure that she had everything, she needed for the first week, he returned to Cincinnati.

He was at home when on Monday afternoon, just after he arrived home from work, the doorbell rang, and two deputies asked if they could ask him a few questions. They asked if they could come in and he escorted them in and asked if they wanted a coke or coffee.

They asked whether he had seen Annie on the day she went missing. He casually lied that he had no idea about her where abouts, and said he was sorry to hear that she was missing. He made the point that she seemed to be a very nice girl and had even brought cookies to his house when he first moved in.

Jeff figured he had about a month before he needed to resupply Annie at the cabin. This would probably be long enough for the search to have died down, but he would make sure to be cautious on the next few trips to the cabin.

He wanted to make Annie happy and to convince her he meant well. He went to the library and found out what topics and books Annie would be taking in school. At twelve he figured she was in seven grade.

He checked up on the math, science, and history that a seventh grader would be taking.

He then went to several bookstores and even a used bookstore to get seventh, eighth and ninth grade self-teaching books.

At the used bookstore he found a treasure. In one set he had Charles Dickens, Jane Austen, Emily Dickinson. He picked up Lewis Carrol, Jules Verne. He spent twenty-five dollars and walked out with over fifteen books. He decided he would save them and take them to the Cabin a few at a time.

All his purchases were in cash.

He settled into a weekly routine that had him at the cabin on weekends and at work throughout the week.

The years had passed quickly. It was a period that he remembered fondly. He took Annie for walks in the woods every weekend. She learned not to try to run away. She seemed content to enjoy the walk and collect various objects.

Her paintings fascinated him. She was naturally skilled and her skills continually and noticeably improved. He had only dared take one of her paintings to his house.

Then Angie had reached maturity. He held off until the day she turned eighteen.

He bought a new bed for the room he turned into the master bedroom. Sex at first was clumsy but it improved over time.

He was now the proud father of two beautiful girls.

He had a very smart and talented wife that he was sure had never come to love him.

As he drove, he thought about what he had to do. He figured that eventually that Black b---- detective would track him down.

He had to get to the cabin, take care of things there and then disappear. He was still pondering how to "take care of things."

He figured he would go to the Northeast, maybe to Washington.

He got to Youngstown and checked into a motel that he had never stayed in. He went to the sports bar next door for a beer. The place had screens everywhere. He sat where he could simultaneously watch basketball, hockey, and baseball. There was a fourth screen that featured soccer. He really didn't care for any of them and would rather have had a bowling tournament to watch. By his third beer a plan was slowly beginning to make sense.

He decided that he would take the girls and move back to the Northwest. He would find a job and set up a new life. He would leave Annie, the love of his life, chained in the cabin but leave a shovel and sledgehammer so she could free herself. It would take her several days to get free and then the anchor would make getting to the nearest town a lengthy affair. She would never be able to find him.

Having solved the problem that was in front of him he paid his bill and retired to get some sleep.

He set his alarm for four in the morning. This would get him to the cabin at sunrise.

It was a little over a two-hour drive. He drove carefully on the way into the cabin. It was a route that he could drive with his eyes closed but it had to be traveled at a numbingly slow speed.

8 Jeff

He drove slowly up to the cabin and turned off his headlights. The sun was just breaking over the mountains to the east. He stopped for a moment to enjoy the beauty of the pink clouds slowly turning a light yellow on their far side nearest the sun. He figured everyone in the cabin would still be asleep.

He then unlocked the trunk and took out a shovel and sledgehammer. Out of habit he walked over to the side of the drive where he always hung his keys to prevent them from getting into Annie's possession. He thought about not leaving his keys at the tree, but he figured it was better to be cautious then be regretful.

He carried the shovel and sledgehammer and left them on the front porch next to the entrance. He figured Annie would find them later as she tried to get free.

He then went in and announced his arrival.

Almost immediately he knew something was wrong. Then he saw the hole in the middle of the cabin. He swore under his breath and rushed out through the back door of the cabin.

The large imposing black van caused him to stop in his tracks.

It was not until he had walked to the side of the van that he realized it was a Cincinnati police van.

How had they beat him to the cabin? How had they even found out about it?

He had several hours head start!? How fast had they driven?

He was in turmoil and deep in his mind an anger that was bitter and black rose like a thundering black cloud spewing lightning and thunder.

He spun on his heal and ran back to his car and again opened the trunk. This time he took out his Remington 760.

His plan had changed dramatically. He was now at war. He loaded four rounds into the magazine with 6 mm bullets. He pumped one into the chamber and added another to the magazine. He was now out to kill the intruders and now he was no longer safe if Annie remained alive.

He then approached the van from the side. He expected it to be empty, but he had to make sure. Once he had checked it out. He looked around and found Angie's wagon and the footprints of two people following the trail heading north. He knew the territory well. It was clear that two people were following the wagon trail. The wagon made a clear and easy trail to follow.

Jeff breathed steadily and easily as he jogged at a fast clip. Once he got to the first camp and realized that Annie was following the stream he knew where she was going to end up. He would take a straight path to where she would most likely be.

He came out of the woods expecting to see the wagon Annie and the two girls. He saw nothing!

Then he recalled seeing a flickering light when he had driven in. At the time it did not register. Now he knew that Annie had almost made it to the entrance road. She had head away from the cabin but for some reason she had made a U-turn.

He took another short cut and this time he came out exactly where he believed Annie to be.

The person between he and Annie was the person he had tried to blow up and this time both she and Annie would die. He would first take out Annie. She would never be able to tell her story. The next shot would be the Black detective.

He raised his rifle and took aim.

Little did Jeff know how wrong his logic was going to prove to be. The fact that she had her back to him gave him the impression that he was in control. There was no way for him to know that his mistake was about to put an end to his perverted fantasies of a new life in the Northwest.

9 Found

lex outran Trey by a good quarter of a mile. She saw the flicker of the fire and at the same time car headlights. She was relieved when the car did not stop. As she got closer, she gave out a warning shout of, "Annie I am a friend, I know your mother.

She watched as Annie stood up and slowly back away. Alex took in the chain still attached to her leg. She reached into her jacket pocket and pulled out the picture of Annie's parents standing to each side of Annie's picture on the fireplace.

Annie kept repeating, "Who are you, who are you?"

Then she saw the picture and fell to her knees with a quiet sob and with tears in her eyes.

She pulled the two girls to her and sobbed as she held the picture. She was going to see her mother.

She allowed the fire of hope to come alive.

It was almost immediately replaced by terror as she looked past the approaching Black woman.

Suddenly Alex saw fear in Annie's face. Instinctively she knew that when she turned, she would see Jeff. When she did, the barrel of his rifle seemed to be a cannon. She was looking directly into a hole that seemed huge but also, she realized it was not aimed at her but at Annie.

Instinctively, she stood up to shield Annie.

Jeff's first shot hit Alex just above her sternum.

She staggered back and fought to keep from passing out. Her brain wanted to turn off, but she fought it and won.

Her gun was in her hand. She turned slightly and she fired twice as Jeff's second shot went through the muscle of her left arm.

She felt no pain.

Her first shot hit Jeff dead center in the heart. Her second shot hit the suddenly raised rifle but went on to take out the side of his head. She thought she had missed as Jeff kept coming toward her.

She was going to shoot again then her mind registered that Trey was repeatedly firing his gun into Jeff's back. This was why Jeff was stumbling toward her.

Jeff then fell forward, flat on what remained of his face.

Alex turned, grabbed the two girls, and ran toward the bridge. This was a sight that she did not want them to see. She fell to her knees as Annie pulled the heavy anchor chain and cement post that had fallen out of the wagon. She finally caught up to the three of them.

Trey caught up to them and pulled off his belt and quickly applied it as a tourniquet to Alex's bleeding arm. He then asked if

Alex had been hit anywhere else. She was finding it hard to talk and just pointed at the center of her chest. She was finding it hard to keep from passing out.

The slug had hit the vest, flattened and stuck to the Kevlar protective jacket.

All Trey said was, "Wow and you nailed him twice after getting hit twice. You had him before I could even get started."

The two girls were asking what was happening.

Annie was still holding them and crying. She could not stop. She had kept control of herself for so many years and suddenly she knew that she was going to be free.

All the years, all the years! Now she was free!

The dam broke and she could not control herself.

Alex crawled over and took Annie in her arms and hugged her. She pulled the girls to the two of them. And told them that their mother was crying because she was happy, and they should just hug her.

Trey let Alex know that he was going to jog up to the cabin and get their van. He had put in a call to the Chief back in Cincinnati and asked him to get help out to where they were located. He let him know that the black transport van would be parked where Annie and Alex were located.

Trey made a point of leaving out the details. He figured that Alex deserved being the one to fill in the details. Her speed had saved Annie; her dead aim had saved them both.

He was constantly being surprised and amazed by his partners toughness.

On his return with the van, he positioned it so that it blocked the view of Jeff's body. Alex's head shot had taken out half of his face. There were no brains left in the cavity. It was a gruesome sight even for Trey, who had seen worse in combat.

Using the first aid kit in the van, Trey stopped the bleeding and bandaged Alex's arm. She now had bandages along her entire left arm. She still had on the bandages from the scrapes she received from getting thrown back by the car bomb blast.

Trey had his own bruises and realized that the explosion had only been the day before.

Trey knew how sore and ache he felt and was amazed that Alex had been able to run for the distance she had and then to take a shot to her chest from thirty feet or so and to be able to return fire. He knew she was going to be sore for weeks. He figured she was the toughest person he knew.

Alex announced that she had eggs, bacon, hot dogs and buns and English muffins and asked what each wanted for breakfast?

"Just tell Trey what you want, he is a great cook," Alex smiled at him as he saluted.

Trey knelt down and listened as the girls decided on what to have for breakfast. He then took them out to gather some wood to make the fire. He talked to them as he gathered the stones for a ring to contain the fire. He was explaining why the fire ring was so important. It was clear to Alex that he was good with children.

Annie sat down next to Alex and asked her name again.

Alex gave her name and at the same time she pulled out her I-phone and dialed Linda, Annie's mother.

She said hello and asked Linda where she was. Linda replied that she was just getting ready to go into work.

Alex told her to go to the couch and sit down. Alex had called via face time, and she watched as Linda's face went white.

"It's good news," Alex quickly blurted out when she realized she had been clumsy with the call.

"Annie would like to talk with you." Alex went on as she gave the phone to an astonished Annie.

For the first five minutes there was only sobbing and crying.

Alex leaned back, she had survived and had saved the person she had been trying to save. She knew she had beat the odds and had won the biggest gamble in her life with a hand that was no more than a pair of twos.

The adrenalin was going down, and the pain was going up.

She was just about to join in on the sobbing due to the pain when the flashing red light of the emergency vehicle and the blue and red flashing police vehicles came across the bridge and out into the clearing.

The lead deputy asked who was in charge. Trey pointed to Alex as she pointed to him. The deputy walked up to her and asked if she was the famous, Cincinnati Black Annie Oakley.

Everything became silent as Alex looked around and shook her head in the affirmative and laughed. She asked who had referred to her by that handle.

The deputy gave a small chuckle and replied that he thought the person was her boss.

During the conversation with the deputy her arm had received a pain shot and the EMT's were patching her up.

Another deputy came back from examining Jeff's body. He asked who had shot the victim from the front and who had shot him from the back.

"I am the back shooter," Treys spoke up. "I wasn't sure if my partner was going to be able to do her thing but as always, she got him before I could."

"Well, I don't think it was a fair fight. You Cincinnati folks seem to be a tough bunch." he went on.

He then told the senior deputy that he had called the coroner and told him to bring the hearse.

The EMTs wanted to take Alex to the local hospital but Alex declined and said that she planned to have two eggs over easy, with a buttered English muffin for breakfast. She also told them she planned to ride back in comfort to Cincinnati and civilization. She thanked them for patching her up.

She told the sheriff and EMTs that if they wanted breakfast, they should let Trey know what they wanted.

The senior deputy came over and apologized but said that he needed them to relinquish their weapons. They would be part of the evidence that would be processed as part of the shooting. The weapons would be returned in a week or so.

The EMT's were continuing to work on her and had removed her Kevlar jacket. They marveled at the fact that she had not passed out when she was hit at such a close range. They conjectured that at such a close range the impact must have been enormous. They pressed on Alex's ribs to make sure none had been broken.

Even with the pain medication Alex groaned when they pressed on her breastbone.

Alex removed her holster and gave it to the deputy.

The woman EMT peered down Alex's blouse and declared that it was impossible to tell the size of the bruise. Alex looked down and laughed.

"Black on black makes it hard to tell doesn't it," she said as she looked at her examiner.

After an awkward moment there was a quiet, "yes it does."

Well, if you have some non-addictive pain medication, I will gladly accept it. I am sure that it is going to hurt tonight and in the morning.

The EMT then came over to Annie and said that they were ready to transport her and the girls to the hospital for examination.

Annie looked at Alex and asked if that was necessary. All that she had needed was the chain removed. Now that it was done she wanted to get home and see her mother as quickly as possible.

Alex smiled and said that she was under arrest and in her custody and would remain with her until they got to Cincinnati.

The local sheriff spoke up and told the EMT's that they could depart.

Alex got up and went over to where Trey was cooking over the campfire and sat next to the two girls. She asked for two eggs, and a buttered English muffin.

She then asked the two if they liked camping.

An hour later after the Jeff's body had been removed, they drove up to the cabin and helped Annie pack up and load her things into the van. There were hundreds of oil, water-color paintings, and a large number of sketch pads.

Alex noted that Annie was a very good artist.

All of Annie's and the girl's belongings easily fit into the van.

It was noon before they were ready to start back toward Cincinnati. She had talked with the Chief, and he had approved of her stopping on the way back.

Alex called ahead to an Embassy Suites in Akron. She planned to sit in the hot tub and then get a good night's sleep and a big breakfast in the morning.

She had her left arm in a sling. The EMT's had removed the earlier bandages. The scrapes on her arm had started to scab over. The EMT's had given her some ointment and told her to keep her arm dry and use the ointment until the healing was complete.

She was left with a bandage on the upper part of her arm.

The ride out of the forest to Youngstown seemed tediously slow. It was clear to Alex that Annie was overwhelmed with emotion. She sat in the seat behind Trey and periodically touched her two daughters and then would silently cry.

Alex had Lorrie come to sit in the front seat and she went back and sat in the bucket seat next to Annie.

She shared some of the details that had followed Annie's disappearance. How each year, her mother and father had pleaded for the abductor to release her. How after five years of continuing to look for leads the lead investigator, now the Loveland Sherriff had closed the case. She mentioned that he was part of the team that helped Alex to find her and that each year he had visited her parents on her missing anniversary day.

And she shared that the case had been reopened because a librarian had come to the station and told her story about a rumor of a woman held in the woods. This was a duplicate story to what Alex's data analysis genius had given to her a few days before.

Annie had many questions about the phone and how amazing it was that she had been able to talk to and see her mother. It had been overwhelming but she thanked Alex for having thrust her into the present so quickly. She wondered what else had changed while she was chained in the cabin in the woods.

Alex replied that technology and medicine had made so much progress that she had no clue what Annie would experience. She advised her to take it one step at a time. She pointed out that both she and the girls would need time to adjust. Alex said that finding her had become personal for both Trey and her. They would be available for Annie to lean on whenever she needed to lean. Alex told her that her friends had fond memories of her and had all wished her luck in closing the case.

Trey conversed with Lorrie and Linda. He told them about the van's cruise control. He turned on the radio and tuned in a rock station. Even Annie was pulled into his banter and the music.

Alex let go and fell asleep. She did not wake up until Trey pulled into the Embassy Suites and loudly announced the arrival. Later she sat in the hot tub with her left arm out on the side and watched as the two girls and Annie played in the pool. The hot water felt marvelous as it washed by her aching body.

Trey had his own room. Alex had decided that she would share one of the larger suites with Annie. She figured there would be some time after the girls went to sleep when Annie would need someone to talk to.

Alex understood that the case had been very personal from the beginning. She was not yet aware of how personal and how rewarding closing the cold case would be. She did, however, thank the hand from above for having guided her in taking the right actions and being at the right place at the right time.

She would close her eyes for the night wondering what the future held for all of them.

10 Home

*A*lex talked with Annie into the late night and concluded that Annie had matured into a well-developed person. She was widely read, had a deep understanding of history, the arts, and events in the past. Alex was sure she would quickly make the adjustment to the changes that had happened since her kidnapping.

Her two daughters would also provide a positive focus. In the near future she would need a job but that was not on the critical path to recovery.

Annie wanted to get a degree from some university. This was one goal that had helped her keep going during her confinement. Having listened to Annie for several hours, Alex believed that any university would be lucky to have her in their student body.

The next morning after taking a pain pill and getting herself ready. Alex helped get the two girls dressed and ready for breakfast. The four of them took their few items and went down for breakfast.

Trey had arrived for breakfast before them and had secured a table big enough for all of them.

He knelt down and gave each of the girls a good morning hug and then said good morning to Annie and her.

Annie and the girls ordered bacon and pancakes and then went to the buffet section and got some fruit.

Annie looked at all the food that the girls had brought to the table and commented that they had more than they would be able to eat for a week.

Alex had waited before getting her own breakfast and volunteered to help. She got a plate and helped herself to some scrambled eggs, some bacon, and an English muffin.

Linda offered her half of her blueberry muffin and Lorie gave her a banana.

Trey was gifted with food from all three that he added to his three waffles dripping in syrup.

The girls sat quietly as they played a game on Alex's and Trey's phones.

She listened as Annie talked about the time, she had been held captive. She pointed out that Jeff had never been mean. He had been very generous and had supplied her with what she asked for. He had wanted her to love him. He never understood that it would never happen.

She commented that she was sad that he had attacked them and been killed. He would probably have killed her, but he would never have harmed the girls.

Annie again thanked Alex for saving her.

Later as they drove back toward Cincinnati, even a rest stop provided the girls and Annie a new experience. Trey asked Alex if it would be OK to stop at a McDonald that had a play center for lunch.

Alex laughed at the request because she had often shared her negative opinion about such places. She reassured him it would be fine.

It was more than fine. Annie and her daughters all frolicked and disappeared under the balls in the ball chamber.

Alex took it all in and wondered if she would do the same with her own kids. She figured that on occasions she would succumb just like all the other parents did.

Alex again called Linda and let Annie and her talk.

The joy-based sobbing dominated the conversation. Everything was ready for Annie's arrival. Word of her return had gotten out and a gathering of her friends were already gathered at the house. They had brought flowers and gifts.

When they drove the black van in, cars filled the street and cul-de-sac near Annie's home. The driveway had been kept clear for the Van.

Alex saw the across the street neighbor standing in the driveway with a plate of cookies.

Alex stepped out first and helped Linda and Lorie out of the van. Annie was surrounded and could barely move.

Trey became the ice breaker and led the way into the house. Annie hugged her dad and then her mom as she got into the house. She introduced her daughters and then knelt to hug her sister and brother. Her mother knelt and hugged her two granddaughters.

Alex noted the situation and signaled for her and Trey to go to the van. They had Annie's father open the garage and proceeded to put all of Annie's belongings along the side wall. The paintings took up the most space.

All the paintings gave Alex an idea. She randomly selected three that she liked. She wrote a note to Annie to let her know she was borrowing three of her paintings.

The next day Alex called an acquaintance that owned an art shop and asked if she was willing to hold an art exhibition for a very talented artist.

Her reply that she was always interested in finding new talent, but she would need to first to see the art and then decide if it was of good enough quality and quantity to hold a showing.

She made an appointment to show her three of more than one hundred paintings, full size sketches and notebook sketches of a new exceptional artist that was about to hit the scene.

She and Trey went into the house and let Linda and Stanley know that they were leaving. They both got hugs and thank-you from both of them. They gave little Linda and Laurie hugs and waved goodbye to Annie who was surrounded by her friends.

Alex wondered if Rob Netherland might be one of the young men that was part of the crowd. She hoped so. He had asked to be called, and she had called him to let him know that she had found Annie.

Annie broke away to give both of them hugs and whispered thank-you. She stepped back and had to wipe tears from her eyes, but she had a beaming smile at the same time.

Alex thought of rain and sunshine and that it usually signaled a very good day.

On the way back to the office Trey pulled off the highway and drove into Graeter's and said that he wanted a coffee ice cream, and he would treat Alex to whatever she wanted.

Alex laughed at the Trey's counter gesture and knew that like herself; he was out of the psychological ditch and once again on firm sober supporting ground.

When they arrived at the office, the Chief and the whole office was waiting for them. It was the weekend, but they had all made it a point to come in to greet them. Trevor pointed to the coffee, rolls, and a big bowl of cut fruit. Bill commented that everyone had heard about the heroic actions the two of them had taken.

The Chief came over to shake hands and congratulate them on having solved the case. He commented that he was the only one lucky enough to have a Black Annie Oakley and a Bat Masterson working together as detectives. This got a cheer and a hurrah from everyone in the room.

Lyndsey and Nolan came and gave both Trey and her a hug. She was happy to hear Nolan call her aunt Alex.

She now had three young people calling her Aunt.

Johnnie stood was standing by quietly. Alex stood up and announced that her magician, miracle analyst had been the one that made the rescue possible. She laughed and declared she had never seen him blush so deeply.

It took a moment before her weak joke was understood.

Matt arrived in his EMT uniform. He was still on duty, but his team had insisted that he had to be there. He came over and tenderly gave Alex a hug.

He looked around and commented that it was official business. He was making sure that Alex had received the proper treatment from those less talented EMTs in Pennsylvania or was that N.Y?

Johnnie let out a controlled "Hurrah!" and everyone applauded.

Alex thanked everyone for having come to the office to welcome them back. She commented that Annie's story was just beginning, and everyone should standby for what would come next.

Bill and Trevor had volunteered to drive Alex to her apartment. She thanked them for offer but said that her bike had been in the rack all weekend and that she was going to take it home.

Not long after, she unchained it and began walking it slowly back to her apartment. She would have loved to ride it, but she was not sure her left arm could handle it.

She had left the three paintings under her desk and would take them on Monday and show them to her art dealer contact.

Johnnie caught up with her and asked to take her bike. He told her she owed him one for embarrassing him in front of entire detective unit.

Alex replied that she was only trying to get him a raise but added that she would bake a sheet of cookies that they could share after they had their lunch pizza on the morrow.

He invited her in for a dinner salad on the today. He leaned her bike on wall outside his apartment and guided her in.

Johnnie wanted to hear about her finding Annie.

Alex began by thanking him for having been so thorough and making the maps that had taken them straight to the cabin. She made the point that without his work she and Trey might have gotten there too late.

As it turned out they were only minutes ahead of Jeff.

She explained that Annie had freed herself and was trying to escape. She now had two young daughters. From her campsites it was clear that she had freed herself early in the week and had tried to get out of the area but had instead made a U-turn that brought her back to within a half mile from where she had started.

She described going through the night as Trey tracked Annie down and then in the early morning seeing a small fire at the edge of a small open area near a creek.

She had run ahead and left Trey far behind.

She approached Annie while unknown to her, Jeff had appeared behind her. He had shot her twice before she got her two shots off. Her replying shots found their marks and Trey, who had arrived at the same time, emptied his gun into Jeff as well. She made the point that Jeff was dead before he hit the ground.

She related the account about the one female EMT's having looked down her blouse to check the area where she had been hit in the chest and realizing that a black and blue bruise would be near impossible to see.

Johnnie commented, "White Folk."

He went on and laughed and commented that it was very much like her blushing joke.

After finishing the salad and bringing Johnnie up to date she took her bike and went up the elevator to her apartment.

She used some plastic wrap to cover the bandage and the rest of her left arm and stood under the shower for almost an hour.

The knock on the door and the person with beautiful green eyes standing there with a red rose answered a wish she had made when she was standing in the shower.

She opened the door and pulled Matt into the apartment. She asked if he had come to hold her so she could have a great night's sleep.

She took the single rose and put it into a tall slender vase.

Matt went into the bathroom and got ready for bed. He got in on his side but Alex asked to change sides so she could put her left arm over him.

She was asleep as soon as she went horizontal in her bed.

Her dreams were of a valley along a gentle stream where she danced with two laughing young girls that caller her Aunt.

10 Home

11 Once in a Lifetime

Her eyes opened and she put up her arm to protect herself. In her morning wake up, she had been reliving her experience when she had been shot.

Matt touched her cheek and whispered that she was safe and that he would get up and fix some breakfast.

She was glad that the Chief had told her to take the next few days off. The internal affairs department would call both her and Trey for interviews. Both of them would have to have a session with the phycologist before they could go back on active duty.

The Chief had then laughed and said that before he could reissue her another weapon, she had to again pass the firearms and shooting test. He warned her not to fail.

She stayed under her warm blanket and slowly thought through the events of the past week and the weekend. It was almost an hour later when she awoke again. She had dozed off and now woke up refreshed and eager to get the day going.

Matt had put breakfast on hold. He poured a cup of coffee for her and asked if two eggs over easy with a butter English muffin would suffice.

He said he had to leave after breakfast because unlike a certain detective that he loved, he did not have the day off.

She thanked him for being around when she needed him.

She let him know what she had planned. He commented that she was truly into trying to have the story have a happy ending.

He gave her a hug and kiss and left for work.

She and Brenda had agreed to meet for lunch at Scoto's.

Alex was looking forward to the lunch meeting. She planned to walk to the office to get the three paintings and take them to the lunch meeting. She hoped that the paintings would make the concept of getting a showing for Annie's paintings a reality.

She was not sure exactly how many paintings they had transported back from the cabin, but it had to be several hundred.

It was clear to her that Jeff had desired to win Annie over. He was willing to buy her all the art supplies Annie desired.

The books that he had purchased were numerous and very educational.

Annie clearly had read them and had educated herself during her captivity. Many of the science and math books that Alex had seen were college level material.

Alex had eaten light. She was saving her appetite for a leisurely and substantial lunch meal.

After breakfast she went down to Johnnie's apartment for another cup of coffee.

She again wanted to thank him. His work had been a key breakthrough.

He opened the door and smiled. He said good morning and told her she had made the day for him.

She gave him a hug and asked if he had a cup of coffee for her. She sat at the kitchen table.

They talked for about an hour at which time Alex told him about meeting with an art dealer acquaintance that owned an art shop and whom she hoped would put Annie's art on display.

She then thanked him for the coffee and left to get the paintings.

When she walked into the work area, it suddenly got quiet. She was glad that Travis was there to break the silence with a snide remark about a plow horse not being able to live out of its harness or was she missing him.

She replied that she had missed him and came in to give him a hug and a kiss.

Since she was walking toward him, he thought she was serious but when she got to her desks she laughed and told him she was just kidding.

The room burst into laughter and Trevor shook her finger at her.

She reached under her desk and pulled out the three paintings. She carefully wrapped and tied them in a large piece of plastic that Johnnie had given her.

"See you all in a few days. I was just practicing coming to work," she said loudly so every could hear her.

It was a pleasant morning, the sun was warm, a light breeze seemed to be pushing her from behind, but it was not strong enough to make it hard to carry the paintings.

She laughed at the feeling of worrying about rejection of the paintings. She was glad they were not hers, otherwise she would have panicked or have cancelled the meeting.

Her willingness to take make the effort to see if she could help Annie would pay off in many more ways than she anticipated.

She continued to take that action that would make her an Aunt to two more children that would see her as their heroine and make Annie a life-long friend.

For Alex it was just the right thing to do. She was a pretty good artist, but Annie was superior in every way.

She was a few minutes early. Scoto's seemed rather empty, but it gave her the chance to select a corner table that would provide plenty of room to set up at least one painting. She arranged the table so she could place one of the pictures on the table and lean it against the wall.

The waiter, who was familiar with Alex as one of the customers that the boss liked, immediately came over and commented how much he liked the painting.

A few moments later Alex waved at the person she only knew as Brenda.

Brenda walked over and the two of them hugged and Brenda reintroduced herself as Brenda Lazenger, proud owner of Lazenger Art LLC.

She looked at the picture and commented that she wished she could paint as well as the artist that had rendered the one, she was looking at.

Alex suggested they order lunch and while they waited for their order, she would show Brenda two more and after lunch they could talk business and next steps.

Alex was glad she was hungry because she could hardly contain herself as Brenda kept commenting on the skill and talent, she saw in the three paintings. She said she would like to meet the artist that had this talent.

After the meal Alex declined desert and was glad that Brenda did as well. She offered to pay for lunch, but Brenda suggested they split the bill.

Brenda then asked what Alex had in mind.

Alex asked if Brenda would evaluate several hundred paintings and provide an estimate of what they might sell for. She went on to say that she had randomly picked the three she had with her but that all the paintings were similar in quality. Alex wanted Brenda to set a price for each piece and arrange an exhibition.

Alex went on and asked about Brenda's fee for doing so.

Brenda looked at the three pictures again. She asked why the artist was not with Alex.

Alex replied that she was sure if Brenda tuned into the news channel, she would learn who the artist was. She went on to say that she did not yet have the artist's permission to offer the paintings for sale. She had hoped that Brenda could provide an honest evaluation about the paintings before raising the hopes of the artist.

"This has to do with the young woman that was abducted years ago, and you must be Cincinnati's Black Annie Oakley!" Brenda blurted out.

"I can't believe my luck," Brenda commented.

She then pointed at the three paintings and said that she could sell them in a heartbeat for at least a thousand a piece and maybe twice that. I usually charge a forty percent fee but, in this case, I only want ten percent and the right to frame them and add the cost of the frame to my portion. I base this on the circumstances and the belief that the other paintings are as good.

Alex grimaced at the Annie Oakley mention and muttered that was a label she would probably live with the rest of her life.

She told Brenda that she would arrange a meeting with Annie and give her a call to let her know if Annie was interested. She would let Brenda know when she could see the rest of the paintings. She asked Brenda if she would prepare the three paintings in the manner that she would show them so she could show them to Annie when they met.

Brenda replied that she would love to do so. The pictures once framed would double in value and in pure beauty. She kept repeating Wow. Wow. This is a once in a lifetime break.

Alex enjoyed the breeze and the sun. She walked slowly back to her apartment thinking on how to proceed.

She was not prepared for the reception of the representatives from all the local, national and a few international news channels. They all crowded around her. Johnnie came out and stood next to her and asked everyone to take a step back.

He took over and managed the interview process by pointing to, and in a few cases calling the reporter by name. Alex was impressed by his composure and glad that he kept the process controlled. She spent half an hour answering the questions she knew she was allowed to answer. She made sure not to reveal names or addresses.

She referred many questions to her boss the Chief of Detectives.

Finally, Johnnie closed the interview and guided her through to the apartment entrance which he locked behind him.

Alex followed him as he guided her to his apartment.

Alex thought Johnnie was going to offer her a drink when he said she needed something stronger than coffee to drink. She smiled and gave him hug when he filled a tall class with ice and poured in a Mountain Dew.

When he asked how the meeting went with the art dealer, Alex replied that it went very well and that she was going to contact Annie to set up a meeting as the next step.

No sooner had she uttered the words when her phone rang. It was Linda, Annie's mother. She said that Annie would like Alex, and her partner to come to dinner. They were to bring their partners or significant others.

Alex replied that she would love to do so. She then asked if it would be possible to meet before that. She shared that she had shown several paintings to an art dealer and potentially the paintings in the garage were worth hundreds of thousands.

Linda thanked Alex for doing so and asked if breakfast the next day was too soon.

Alex replied that the timing was perfect.

The rest of the day seemed to take forever. Matt had the evening shift, but he was happy to agree to dinner at Annie's.

The next morning seemed to take forever to arrive.

Alex got up, arranged for an Uber, and took her last bag of Ghirardelli chocolate with her. She was going to give them to the girls.

Her arrival at Annie's home brought four young children running to greet her.

All of them called her Aunt Alex.

She knelt and got a hug from all of them. She gave the chocolate to "old" Linda and told her that she and Annie would need to control the candy flow to the kids.

Annie came to her and gave her a hug and again thanked her for bringing her out of the woods and back home.

Alex acknowledged the thanks but said that from now on they would just meet as good friends.

Linda guided them to the kitchen table and instructed the kids to go to the basement and play. She showed them the individually wrapped candy and promised them it would be part of their morning treat. It was effective in getting all of them out of the kitchen.

Linda asked how long Alex could stay. She went on to explain that Stanley was already at work and that she had taken Monday off but today she was scheduled in by ten. She would take her two and drop them off at day care.

Alex understood what was being said and being asked. Linda did not want to leave Annie alone. To Alex it was somewhat ironic. Annie had managed alone, anchored by an ankle chain for almost fifteen years. She had been very much alone.

She had raised her two girls to be well-mannered and behaved.

She reflected that it was indeed like a mother to worry about her daughter even when they had developed into well-functioning adults.

Alex answered that she had the whole day in fact she had the whole week!

Annie insisted on cooking Alex breakfast. She promised that there were no hotdogs for breakfast this morning.

Alex liked her attitude and ordered two over easy, toast and jam and a cup of black coffee.

After Linda left with her two. Little Linda and Lorie came into the kitchen and sat down with a book that Linda read to Lorie.

After taking her breakfast dishes to the sink and rinsing them Alex broached the subject of the showing and selling her paintings.

Annie commented that the paintings had been her means of keeping her sanity. They had been a release of emotion, fear, and a long cry into the unknown.

She had mixed feelings about selling them, but they seemed to represent a way to buy her future and the future of her children.

Alex recognized the number when the phone rang. She put the conversation on the speaker phone. Brenda immediately asked if Alex had contacted the artist. Alex replied that she was on the speaker phone with the painter.

Brenda went hurriedly on to say that she had grossly underestimated the value of the paintings. She had contacted her appraiser and shown him the paintings and given him a brief history of the artist.

He immediately said the paintings were worth ten times the estimate that she had given.

He told me to call immediately and clarify the situation.

He went on to say that he could arrange a showing that would be global. With a little bit of advertising the paintings would be bid on by thousands of art lovers. He predicted that the paintings might be worth somewhere between five hundred thousand to one point five million.

Alex was watching Annie's face. The impact was clear. She thanked Brenda for the call and was in the process of hanging up.

Brenda blurted out, "Wait! I have a request or question."

When can I do an inventory and evaluation of this treasure?

Alex looked at Annie and asked when Brenda could come out.

Annie quietly said anytime. Today at two would be fine with me. My two will be taking a nap and it will give me a chance to be with Brenda as she looks over my life via my paintings.

Alex said she would text Brenda the address.

Alex hung up and asked Annie about her feelings at being recognized as an artist with extremely high skill and talent.

Annie looked at her and asked if Alex always moved at lightning speeds.

This made Alex smile. She replied that her boss thought she rushed in where angels feared to tread.

Yes, she replied that once she had an idea, she acted on it as fast as she could. This meant her mistakes were usually superseded by a good outcomes.

Alex asked whether public exposure felt threatening?

Annie took a long drink of her coffee. Then replied that she was not afraid of fame and fortune, but she really wanted to concentrate on Linda and Lorie and make sure they had a smooth transition into a fun childhood. She would skip the fame and fortune if it got in the way.

Alex replied that for next several months she would be sought out, invited to speaking engagements, asked to write a book and most likely to parties by people she did not know. She went on to say that it would be fairly intense and that she should make choices based on her feeling at the time.

She suggested that Annie get an agent that would shield her from the coming storm. She asked if Annie knew anyone.

Annie laughed and replied that yes, she had been approached many times when she was chained in the cabin.

Alex grinned and agreed that all those visitors coming to the cabin probably had overwhelmed her. She went on to say that a good friend of hers could help her find such a person.

She then asked about the dinner invitation. She would like to invite her significant other and the person that would help find the agent she was suggesting.

Annie replied that anyone that Alex identified was welcome.

Alex thanked her and then suggested that the dinner should be catered and asked what Annie had in mind.

Annie replied that she and her mother had planned on doing the cooking. At the moment she had no money, and she knew that her parents could not afford a catering service.

Alex replied that she would pay for the dinner and Annie and her mother could select the menu. One painting would more than pay for it. Besides, if Annie would become famous then the painting would be worth much more than the dinner.

Annie replied that Alex could have as many paintings as she wanted and that getting the dinner catered would make it much easier on her and her mother. She suggested that they go to the garage, and she find the one she had in mind..

Annie took the two girls by the hand and said that they could play in the backyard. She commented to Alex that she had a hard time letting the girls out of her sight, but the backyard was enclosed with a six-foot high fence and the only way in or out was through the garage.

Annie took the first picture and showed Alex the date that it had been painted and a comment about what it meant to her. This information was neatly printed on the canvas behind the frame where the wrapped around.

Alex continually commented on her reaction to each painting. As the two of them put the paintings in date order, Alex could see the artist improving. The first third of the paintings were very good, the second third were great, the last third were clearly an artist that had exceptional talent. The three paintings that Alex had taken to show Brenda belonged in the first third.

Alex commented on this fact that she saw the improving skill. The three she had taken to show Brenda were all in the early years or the first third. She hoped Brenda would recognize this.

It was clear to Alex that the sales goal should be adjusted to the high end.

Alex worked with Annie organizing the paintings for about an hour when Linda and Laurie came into the garage and said they were hungry.

Annie asked what they would like for lunch and they both said they wanted a hot dog. Annie looked at Alex and said that it was her and her partner's fault that the girls had latched onto the hot dog as their favorite for all meals.

Alex bowed her head, smiled, and replied that it was her favorite as well.

The four of them left the garage and headed for the kitchen.

Alex looked back and realized that her estimate of the number of paintings had been low. There were probably twice the number she had given to Brenda. She wondered what her reaction would be to both the quantity and the ever-improving quality.

Annie admitted that she too liked hot dogs that were smothered with chopped onions, relish, and lots of catsup. Her hot dogs needed to be eaten with a fork and knife. She went on to say that she like to use multigrain buns that she made. She had baked a dozen buns the day before and that hot dogs would make an easy quick lunch.

Alex worked her way slowly through her lunch. She chatted with Linda and Lorie and asked them how they liked meeting their grandmother and grandfather.

The two said it was great. They also said that they liked their mom's little brother and sister and that is was weird that they were their "aunts." They asked what they should call Alex.

Alex was about to answer when Annie suggested that they call her Aunt Alex. That would make all three of them "Aunts." The two girls giggled and said, Yes, Aunt Alex.

Alex smiled and said that being called Aunt Alex really sounded good.

The doorbell made them all stop talking. Alex got up and said that she would answer. She felt for her firearm and realized that she was currently not allowed to have one.

She looked through the side pane and opened the door when she saw it was Brenda.

Brenda looked at her watch and then said good afternoon.

Annie stepped to Alex's side, introduced herself, and invited Brenda in. She introduced Linda and Laurie and then asked who would like some cookies and coffee or a glass of milk.

Alex set the tone by accepting a cookie and a cup of black coffee. The two girls eagerly said milk and cookies. Brenda got the hint and accepted a cup of coffee with cream, no sugar and one cookie.

Annie brought in the coffee and cookies with three cups of coffee. She excused herself and took Linda and Lorie into the kitchen.

Alex could hear Annie instruct the two to enjoy the cookies and milk in the kitchen then afterwards they should go to the basement to read. They were to let her, or Aunt Alex know when they went to the basement.

Alex was impressed with how Annie handled the girls.

Annie came back into the living room and brought up the subject of her paintings. She boldly went on to ask why she should have Brenda handle the showing and sales of her paintings.

It was clear to Alex that Brenda had not expected such a direct and challenging approach.

Brenda took a bite of her cookie and a sip of her coffee. She closed her eyes and said that the chocolate chip cookie was the best she had ever tasted.

Then she looked at Annie and replied that she should handle the sales and distribution because she had a strong network and the ability to sell internationally. She herself was a painter and knew fine art when she saw it. The work that Alex had shown her was exceptional.

She went on to make a joke that she should be the one that Annie chose otherwise she would have to come to the door begging for another cookie.

She stopped talking, smiled, and reached for an oatmeal-raisin cookie.

Annie smiled and said that since she came recommended by Alex and she had complimented her cookies they should go out to the garage and see if Brenda would continue to feel she should be the one to handle the paintings.

Annie stood up and looked at Alex and asked if she would mind staying in the house with the girls.

Alex nodded in the affirmative, but she took a moment to share her viewpoint. She told Brenda that the estimate of the number of paintings she had given her was low and the pictures she had brought for her to see were on the low end of the quality she would see in the garage.

She closed by asking to be involved in any financial agreements.

Annie replied that she would wait until later to discuss any financial arrangements. First, she wanted to hear from an art dealer whether she would go through the hassle to expose her personal life to the public.

She turned and led the way out to the garage.

Alex carried the remaining cookies and the empty cups into the kitchen. She rinsed the dishes and put them into the dishwasher.

She took three raisin-oatmeal cookies and went into the basement. The excited reaction from Linda and Lorie were all she needed to make it a great day.

She found a Hooks and Ladder game and the three of them sat on the floor playing.

Alex was engrossed in laughing and playing with the girls and did not hear Annie come down the stairs.

Annie watched quietly for a few moments and then announced that playtime was over, and everyone should come upstairs and get ready for Grandmother Linda to come home.

Alex could tell by the expression on Abbie's face that the time in the garage had gone well. She helped the girls put away the game and then brought up the rear as they all went up the stairs.

Abbie asked if Alex wanted to stay for Mac and Cheese, broccoli, and a small cut of roast beef.

Alex thanked her but declined. She was ready for the treadmill and a quiet evening reading and just relaxing. She thanked Annie for the hospitality and said she was looking forward to the Friday evening dinner. She reminded Annie that she was paying but Annie and her mother were responsible for selecting the caterer and the menu.

Before leaving she inquired on how Brenda had reacted to the paintings in the garage.

Abbie, first thanked Alex for connecting her with a way that she could be financially comfortable with the future.

She and Brenda had gotten along fine. Brenda had been overwhelmed and said she would like to come back for the next few days so she could finish the inventory. She also said that her initial financial estimate was most likely on the low side. She would come back with it more clearly defined once she had her appraiser friend look them over.

She also made the point that most likely the art would pull in several million. Brenda qualified her estimate by stating that the money would not all come in at once but that there would be an initial surge and then it would come in more slowly as the paintings were hung and other people noticed them and wanted one of their own. She also offered her painting studio for me to work in. She made the point that there was no hurry on her part and that the offer would remain open indefinitely.

Alex had called an Uber and had monitored its arrival. She gave the two girls a hug and thanked them for playing with her.

The opportunity that Alex had created for Annie was more than she had dreamt of. She had closed a cold case and had opened a future that was beyond what she ever imagined. The surge of positive energy was a reinforcement that would in the near future would guide her action leading to her own survival.

12 Dessert

*A*lex closed her eyes and relaxed in the seat of the Uber as she returned to the apartment. She paid her driver and gave him a good tip.

She was about to take the elevator then decided to knock on Johnnie's door. She wanted to invite him to the Friday night dinner.

She said hello, declined an invitation for coffee and dinner. She told him she needed at least an hour on the tread mill. She mentioned the dinner on Friday evening and asked if he would go. She said that he could ride with Mathew and her. His smile and thanks for the invitation gave her a good feeling.

She then took the elevator up to the sixth floor. She dropped off her purse, changed into her running outfit, and went down to the gym.

Once she was in rhythm on the treadmill, she called Mathew. It was great to hear his voice and the clear appreciation that she had called. They chatted for a while then Alex asked if he would like to share a salad, and a bottle of wine. The idea had come on its own volition. Mathew replied that he thought she would never ask. He had figured that maybe she had dropped him.

Alex gave a small laugh and wondered if she had been so negligent. She replied that no, he was constantly on her mind, and it was too bad they could not communicate mind to mind. If they had been able, he would constantly be blushing.

She finished the hour and then went back up to the apartment. She took a shower and then went to the kitchen to make a lettuce, tomato, cucumber salad with chunks of cheese, and smoked salmon. She sprinkled on some olive oil and then put in a half cup of vinegar. She mixed the lot and then put it in the fridge. She took out a bottle of alcohol-free Pinot Grigio and put it in the fridge next to the salad.

She set the table and then went into the bedroom and straightened it out. She was not sure what would transpire but she was ready for however the evening progressed.

She was ready for an evening with Mathew.

She sat down with a book, but her mind kept going back to Abbie and the two girls. This was a case that that had become personal, and she felt very good about it.

She would need to rethink the sage advice about not letting a case get personal. She would need to be selective about a case that was allowed to be personal.

She then placed a call to Trey to remind him of the dinner on Friday. He replied that he would not miss it. He had gotten an invitation to have the whole family come to the dinner.

Alex was pleased that Abbie had recognized that Trey had a young boy the same age as her two girls.

She then placed a call to the Chief and invited he and his wife to the Friday night dinner. He replied that the two of them would not miss it. He wanted to hear about the rescue from the rescued viewpoint.

He shared the news that he had gotten the council to appropriate the funds for a new car. He had to do some arm twisting but none of the decision makers wanted to be the ones that said no and then be found out in public that they had said no.

The doorbell rang and Alex put her book, still unopened on the living room table. She looked at the title, "Life: What you do on the way to the next adventure." This was her third try at reading the book. Unfortunately, it probably would never get read. She was having too much fun and fulfillment on her current adventure. She didn't need anyone to inspire her for the next one.

She opened the door, pulled Mathew in. She looked into his beautiful green eyes and gave him a resounding kiss as he tried to keep the flowers, he had in his hand from getting crushed and his bottle of wine from dropping out of his hand.

Once he was free from Alex's embrace, he smiled at her and suggested she go into the woods more often.

He put the bottle of wine on the kitchen island and laid the flowers next to it. He then took her into his arms and quietly said they should try it again.

Alex placed the bottle that Mathew had brought next to the one she planned to have with the dinner salad.

She looked at Mathew gave him a deep smile and told him that his bottle would be opened after dessert.

"Can't wait," he replied quietly but with a wide smile.

Mathew complemented Alex on the salad and the exquisite smoked salmon that she had chosen to top it off. He looked into the serving bowl and asked if she wanted any more. When she declined, he ate the remainder from the serving bowl.

After clearing the table and putting the dishes in the dishwasher, Alex took her wine glass, emptied the last bit, and declared it was time for dessert.

She took Mathew's hand and led him to the bedroom. She had chosen this particular apartment building because of its spacious master bedroom.

When her apartment on the fourth floor had been blown up, she had chosen to stay because of this one feature. She had been pleased that she did not have to pay extra for the roof deck access that came with her new sixth floor apartment.

She turned to face Mathew and gave him another deep kiss and then proceeded to slowly take his clothes off. She stopped and embraced and kissed him after taking off each item. When she had taken all of his clothes off. She guided his hands to her blouse and asked him to help her out of her clothes.

Dessert lasted for a little over an exquisite hour. It was slow, easy, and it made her think of honey dripped over chocolate and caramel.

Alex got up and got out her black robe and handed Mathew a matching one. She declared that it was a birthday gift. She helped him put it on as he reminded her his birthday was six months away.

She led him to the couch and asked him if he wanted a glass of the wine he had brought. She was glad he had remembered to select an alcohol-free wine that she too could enjoy.

Alex chose to share her experience about finding Annie and then the discovery of the fortune in paintings that she had painted.

They talked until close to midnight.

She invited Mathew to stay. He let out a small groan. He replied he really would like to, but his shift started at five in the morning.

He smiled and accepted the shower Alex offered. She logically pointed out that he would need one before going work.

The hot water added to the steam that transpired.

Alex dried Mathew off and he returned the favor.

It was close to one when Alex closed her eyes and fell asleep.

She came awake to the incessant buzz of her phone. She sat up on the edge of the bed when she heard Annie's voice.

It was clear to Alex that Annie was in a panic. She asked Annie to stop and begin again and to go slowly.

Annie started crying. She said that she was counting on Alex to help. She said she would call back in a few minutes when she could control her emotions and stop crying.

Alex said she had no clue what was happening, but that Annie could count on her and that together they would solve any problem facing them.

Alex got up and quickly got ready to face the day. The call had her on edge, but she went through her morning ritual of boiling two eggs and getting the toast spread with butter. She chose to put honey on it as well.

She was trying to imagine what might possibly have upset Annie.

The phone rang and Annie was on the line. She apologized about her breaking down on the previous call. She went on to say that she had received a call from a lawyer that represented Jeff's mother and that they were going to go to court to get custody of the two girls.

Annie asked if Alex could help.

Alex thought for a moment and then replied that she would certainly help. She asked if Annie's parents had a lawyer. When Annie replied no, Alex said she had one in mind that handled such cases. She would get this lawyer engaged.

She went on to tell Annie to call Sheriff Evan and let him know and ask him to set up some drive by surveillance to make sure no strange cars came into the neighborhood.

Alex promised to call once she got things organized on her end.

She told Annie to remain calm and that no one would take Linda and Laurie.

A few minutes later Johnnie looked surprised when he opened the door. He invited Alex in and asked her what was up.

Alex explained the situation confronting Annie and said there was work for him to do. Alex asked him to research Jeff's parents. She wanted to know every detail of their lives. If they got a ticket for spitting on the sidewalk, jay walking, a traffic ticket she wanted to know. She would like to have this information as soon as possible.

Then she asked for a cup of coffee and asked if she could sit at the table and make a few calls.

Her first call went to Trey to let him know what was happening. Her second call went to the Chief. He had a few choice words about the boldness of Jeff's parents. Alex asked him who the best lawyer for this case might be.

He volunteered the lawyer's name and said they had been friends for years. He was sure that he could get him to represent Annie.

Johnnie came back into the room with a wide grin and said it was over before it had a chance to begin. Jeff's father had been arrested for drunk driving. His mother was an alcoholic that been in a bar fight.

Alex thanked him for the good news but asked him to do his normal thorough job and dig even deeper. She asked him to trace each parent back to their high school days.

Alex called Annie and let her know that a quick search on Jeff's parents had surfaced information that would get them disqualified in any court contest.

She then asked Annie if she would like to go shopping for her own I-phone and see what might be of interest at the Kenwood Mall.

When Annie agreed, Alex said that she would come by and pick the three of them up and take them to lunch.

She figured the three of them would love the food court.

They would be amazed by the Apple Store and most probably overwhelmed by the mob of people.

Alex had refrained from asking the best lawyer she knew, her mother. She did not want her bias to blind her to what was best for Annie. She would make sure that Linda and Laurie would be raised by the person who had risked everything and was willing to bypass any personal gain to make sure they experienced a normal life.

13 The Mall

On the way to pick up Annie and the girls, Alex got a call from her mother. Her mother accused Alex of having forgotten her parents.

Alex said that perhaps she was somewhat guilty. She went on to describe the events of the past week and how it had overwhelmed her.

Her mother, the best lawyer she knew, had come to her mind when Annie called about the notification from Jeff's parent's lawyer, but she had not wanted to ask for her help. She knew she would get it if she asked.

When her mother understood the situation, she immediately said she would help and asked why Alex had not asked sooner.

Her mother volunteered her help, pro bono. She asked if she might talk to Annie.

Alex told her mother she was on the way to pick Annie up to go shopping. She would give her a call back as they drove to the mall. She could talk to Annie then.

When the Uber arrived, Annie was sitting on the porch swing with the two girls. It was clear to Alex that this outing was a special event for the three. They were dressed in what Alex called their Sunday best. Alex had worn a simple all black pants suit. She usually wore a similar outfit when on duty. Since she carried a revolver, she chose to wear a black jacket. This day she did not need the jacket.

Before she got out to greet the three, she made sure the driver understood not to leave and that all of them were going to Kenwood Mall.

She turned as the girls jumped up and ran to her as they called her Aunt Alex. She knelt and gave them both a hug. She enjoyed being called Aunt Alex by the two girls.

When she called an Uber, she had specified an SUV. She had ridden in the front seat on the way out from her apartment but now she got into the back. The two girls sat in the very back and she and Annie sat in the captain chairs. The driver had provided water, and he offered suckers to the two girls.

Alex smiled as he handed them back. He had just earned a nice tip.

As they drove out Alex explained to Annie that her mother had volunteered to represent her and that her mother wanted to talk with her to figure out the best way to handle the situation.

As she got her mother on the phone Alex explained that her mother was licensed to practice in almost all the states in the Midwest.

She had dialed her mother on a video call. Annie looked at the phone and said to Alex's mother, "wow you and Alex could be sisters."

Alex leaned back and listened, but she knew Annie had given the perfect complement to her mother.

As they talked Annie extended an invitation to her mother to the Friday night dinner. She heard her mother reply that she wouldn't miss it.

Alex got her phone back and had to listen to her mother comment, "See, Annie knows how to treat a mother. She invites them to have dinner."

Alex replied that she was really happy that her mother was so flexible at such a young age.

They both had a good laugh.

Annie looked at Alex and asked if everything was OK.

Alex replied that she and her mother were always playing the poor mother, ungrateful daughter game. It was their way of keeping things light.

The mall as usual was crowded. It felt luxurious to arrive in an Uber. Alex paid via her phone. The driver gave his card as he thanked her for a generous tip. He said he would be pleased to pick them up when they were done.

Alex took the card, thanked him, and let him know that she would indeed call him.

The mall was an instant hit. Alex watched and enjoyed the reaction after reaction from mother and daughters.

She took them to the map of the maul at the top of the entrance incline. She had thought of taking them to the Cheesecake Factory, but she felt that for their first visit, the food court would be a more engaging and interesting lunch area. She decided to save The Cheesecake Factory for their next outing.

The escalator down to the food court enthralled the two girls.

Alex kept being surprised by what she took for granted. She began to see the amazing world around her through the eyes of two young girls. Their world had changed from a dense forest of trees and the animals that called it home to a dense mall that was populated by a large number of people that roamed it.

She accompanied the three as they visited each of the food sources around the food court. She suggested they pick three things that they could all share.

The selections turned out to be a Hawaiian pizza, a Whopper and Chipotle wrap.

Alex picked a table near the wall in which to sit. This gave them the view of the entire food court.

Annie thanked her for bringing them to the food court to have lunch. It was amazing to her. Linda and Laurie chimed in "amazing."

Alex felt gratified to be having such an enjoyable learning experience. She thought to herself that this was one case that she was pleased to have gotten so deeply engaged in.

They each sat munching on a fourth of a delicious pizza, a fourth of a whopper and a fourth of a Chipotle wrap.

Alex enjoyed both the quiet moments and the ones where the girls reacted to the sight of a person with purple hair or some guy or woman going by covered in tattoos.

The meal ended with the girls only eating part of their share. Annie began to say something about them finishing up their food.

Alex put her hand on Annie's arm and quietly asked her if she wanted fat daughters. Annie replied, "Of course not."

The girls cried out, "no fat daughters," and giggled.

Alex declared lunch over and everyone was going to go to the Apple store to buy a phone. She stood up, gathered the girl's food, put it in on the tray, and took it to the trash.

The ride up the escalator provided another moment of excitement for the girls. Annie again thanked Alex for bringing them to the mall.

Alex replied that she was seeing the world around her through the girl's eyes and said no thanks was needed. The girls were providing a huge reward.

The Apple Store caused a momentary hush among the four. The hustle and bustle was overwhelming. The lights and the computers all came together to stop them all in their tracks.

Alex was always overwhelmed when she came to the Apple showroom. She stood a few moments at the entrance to let Annie, and the girls adjust.

She was approached by an Apple "genius" and asked if she needed help or had an appointment.

Alex gave the young lady her name and appointment time.

She was led to an empty seat at the "Genius" bar.

Annie asked if it was always so busy.

Alex replied that it would get worse later in the afternoon right after work.

She turned as she was asked how she could be helped.

She introduced Annie and said that they wanted the latest I-phone, a protective case and also to be set up with training classes on how to utilize the phone.

They were shown the latest phone on the market. Alex asked about colors, and they were shown a pink, a white, lime green and a black one.

Alex looked at Annie and asked which one suited her. Annie picked the black one and chose a black protective case.

Alex watched as the "genius" expertly snapped it together and turned it on. He asked Annie a series of questions and put settings into the phone. He then handed it to Annie and declared it ready for use. He asked when she wanted to schedule the training sessions or if she was not sure he gave her a card that explained how to select the training sessions on-line.

Annie replied that she did not own a computer, but her mother did, and she would figure out how to handle the training appointments.

Alex now knew what gift she was going to bring to the dinner the following night.

On the way out she stopped and asked Annie to wait a moment and that she had forgotten to ask their genius a question.

She went back and asked him to select a laptop that a novice could easily grasp and made the point that she was not looking for the least expensive. She would be back in an hour to see what he had selected. She let him know that she would like it working and ready to go and she empathized that it should be the one he thought would be the best one.

Alex called the Uber driver as she walked out to the front of the store.

When Annie asked what was next, Alex suggested they call an end to the outing and plan another adventure on Saturday or Sunday. She suggested a movie and lunch at The Cheesecake Factory.

She asked Annie if she could go back to her mother's house on her own. The same driver would take them back.

Annie agreed that it would be a better arrangement than Alex going out and coming back the same way.

Alex instructed the driver to take Annie and the girls back to where he had picked them up.

She gave him a time to pick her up the following day at six pm at the same address he had today. He would have three passengers to take to the same address.

He replied that he would be pleased to do so.

Alex paid him for the trip to Annie's house.

Then she gave each of the girls a hug and told them she would see them for dinner on the following day.

Once the car had left, she went back to the Apple Store to buy Annie a laptop.

She knew that the phone and computer would open up a new world for Annie.

She called Matt and asked if he wanted to have an early dinner at the Cheesecake Factory.

He replied that he liked the desserts there, but they paled in comparison to the desserts she served in her apartment. He said he was willing to suffer and have a dose of each.

Alex replied that perhaps that a second dessert at her place might happen sometime on the weekend.

She walked the Mall deciding on the stores to visit the next time she brought Annie and the girls to the mall.

Her continuing involvement with the three persons she had freed was enriching her life. It would continue long after many subsequent cases branded her with new physical and mental scars.

The future would grace her, and she was destined to be a great Aunt.

14 Dinner

lex was reviewing the news on her phone when it vibrated in her hand. It was her mother calling to let her know that she would be in Cincinnati by noon. Her flight would arrive at eleven and she would take a cab to the apartment.

The conversation was short, and it got Alex rolling. She spent part of the time cleaning and washing her clothes. Then she took a shower and made a fresh pot of coffee. She thought about what to have for lunch and decided on lamb, spaghetti, grilled asparagus spears and a mixed salad.

She called Johnnie and invited him to lunch. He gladly accepted and commented it was a special day. He would not have to cook at all.

The lamb chops were frozen and individually wrapped. She had purchased a package of eight, seasoned them and then put them in the freezer. This let her prepare them one at a time when she was cooking for herself.

She followed a similar practice with the salmon and other meats. She could have a full course meal ready in less than a half-hour.

She got her fish pre-seasoned and packaged at Kroger and they only took fifteen minutes. It was a dream way to get a good meal in a hurry with a minimum of work.

It fit her lifestyle.

She ate well but had great control on keeping the calories in check.

When the doorbell rang, she had everything ready to go. The table was set, the bottle of wine in the fridge and the apartment was mother ready.

She opened the door expecting to greet her mother.

It was Johnnie. He said hello and then asked, "Am I too early? You look disappointed."

Alex gave him a hug and replied that he was right on time and that her mother was late.

"Late for what," her mother said as she walked up behind Johnnie, and asked Alex was doing hugging such an old man," she went on as she gave Alex a hug.

She turned to Johnnie and gave him a hug as well and then walked into the living room area.

Alex pulled Johnnie into the apartment and closed the door.

She pointed at the dining table and said she was ready to serve lunch.

Johnnie asked if he could help as he moved to the table. Her mother took his hand and walked him to the table. She told him it was probably better it they both got out of the way.

Alex put the lamb chops on a plate. The grilled asparagus next to it. She put the spaghetti in marinara sauce into a bowl. She brought all to the table and put a serving utensil with each. Finally, she poured the wine and sat down.

She raised her wine glass and made a toast, "to my favorite mother" they clinked glasses and began serving themselves.

Her mother asked her to tell her about how she had managed to solve a cold case that had been closed for almost a decade and that had years of someone trying to solve it.

Alex pointed to Johnnie and told her that he was one of the main reasons she had been able to close the case.

He had been one of the first to bring the case to her attention.

The second person was a librarian that had come into the station to report a strange story she had been told.

The third person was the Loveland Sheriff. He had been a young Loveland deputy on the case and was the one that eventually closed the case years ago.

Each had contributed.

She and Trey had been the blade and the point of the spear on the ground participants.

They had expected to find the remains of a decomposed body but were blessed to find Annie alive and with two daughters.

"I am now officially, Aunt Alex to them" Alex said with a smile and raised her wine glass for another toast.

She went on to explain that the only downside to finding them was the confrontation with Jeff. He must have decided that his only recourse was to kill Annie and take the kids.

Alex described her action of standing up and getting hit dead center in the chest by the shot meant for Annie. The second shot was meant for her, but Trey shot Jeff in the back and the shot grazed my arm. She recounted that she was on the verge of passing out when her two shots hit Jeff in the chest and then between the eyes. He was dead even as Trey continued to fire his gun because Jeff stumbled towards me with his rifle still in his hands.

She described that she had grabbed the two girls and had run as far as she could carry them to prevent them from being traumatized by Jeff laying on the ground with an empty skull. Her second shot literally blew his brains out of his head. Alex admitted that she went weak from the loss of blood from my arm. Trey stopped the bleeding and called for help.

She shared that the best part of that trip was stopping on the way back and staying in the Embassy Suites. The two girls were fun to watch. Everything was a new discovery. It made her realize how many wonderful things she have taken for granted.

"That includes my mother," Alex smiled and raised her wine glass once again.

She let her mother know that she and Trey were both currently official desk duty for the next two weeks. Both of them would have to talk to a psychologist, get cleared by internal affairs and then pass their gun handling test.

She let her mother know that the chief told her to take it easy and let her arm heal.

She went on to share her trip to the maul with Annie and the kids to have lunch and to get a new phone for Annie. The outing was a great success for all of them.

Alex shared that she thought that Annie was a great mother and Linda, and Laurie were great kids. Alex admitted that she thought that she had more fun than they did.

"Well, I think I am talking too much," Alex finished and emptied her wine glass.

Her mother replied that it was more than she usually got from her daughter.

She went on to say that it was a fascinating story. Tell me what you know about Jeff's parents. They seem determined to get custody of the girls. I don't think they have a chance, and I will make sure they don't get close. I have already arranged for a judge to sign a cease-and-desist order that keeps them from coming closer than 100 yards to Annie and the girls. I have also drawn up a counter suit that is designed to keep them from ever contesting this case in their home state of Idaho. They will be lucky to be able to get to Cincinnati any time in the near future.

Johnnie gave a chuckle and commented that he worked for the Black Cincinnati Annie Oakley and was friends with her mother Clarissa Darrel for the defense.

He went on to explain that Jeff's mother and father met in a saloon in Newport, Idaho. Jeff's father was a heavy drinker as was his mother. She had started out in Puget Sound as a stripper and moved to Idaho after several arrests for prostitution and drunken behavior.

Her life in Newport, Idaho tamed down after she married and had Jeff. She was a good mother, still drank too much but Jeff's home life was relatively normal. Both parents cared for him and encouraged him to go to college. He wasn't interested and chose to become a car mechanic.

Alex looked at her mother and asked if Clarissa Darrel had enough information to mount a defense.

Her mother smiled and said yes it certainly seemed so. She asked if she could use the computer so she could prepare a document to present to the Jeff's parent's lawyer.

Alex went to the second bedroom that was set up as an office and activated her computer. She left the room as her mother sat down and opened her briefcase.

She went back into the kitchen where Johnnie was putting the dishes into the dishwasher. She thanked him for being so thoughtful.

He replied that he was impressed with Alex for being so active even as she recovered from a bullet wound. She replied that the arm was not as bad as the chest bruise from the impact of the bullet that hit her there. Her bullet proof vest had done its job, but the result was a double hand sized bone deep bruise.

She commented that her butt was still sore from the car bomb explosion that had thrown her through the air.

Johnnie got done with dishes and said he was going to go back to his apartment and relax until it was time for them to go to dinner.

Alex called Matt, said good afternoon, and chatted for a few moments.

Then she sat down to listen to the news.

Her mother came out of the office bedroom and helped herself to a cup of coffee. She sat down on the couch, took a sip of coffee, and asked how things were working out with Matt..

Alex looked at her mother and smiled and replied that he seemed to be the one. He did not try to dominate or be in charge. She said that they had a hot relationship.

She told her mother that she could get her own impression at dinner in the evening. She explained that he had planned to drive all of them to dinner, but she had convinced him it would be more enjoyable if they all went together in a taxi that a she had arranged.

Alex let her mother know that they were going up early so that they could all see the girls and spend a little time with them before dinner.

Her mother responded that it sounded like a good plan. She was sure there would be some wine flowing since she was bringing three bottles. She went on to point out that Alex's favorite was alcohol free.

She commented that she also had have a gift for the two girls. It's not much but I saw two teddy bears and they came to mind.

She got up and opened up her small suitcase and took out a light tan and a darker one that was about the size of a loaf of bread.

Alex smiled and said it looked a lot like the bear that was on her bed at the moment. She asked if her mother remembered giving it to her.

"Mothers don't forget," was the simple reply.

The two spent the short period before getting ready to go to dinner reminiscing about Alex's childhood and more recently her time in Cincinnati.

Alex enjoyed the time. It had been a long time since she and her mother had spent a significant amount of time together and just talked.

Matt's arrival broke the mother-daughter interlude and started the mother potential son-in-law phase.

Alex was happy to see the two get along so well. She had called the taxi driver and saw on her phone that he was a few blocks away.

She called down to Johnnie and then gathered her gifts. She asked Matt to carry the laptop. He had brought flowers and a bottle of wine as gifts.

It was the same driver that had taken her the day before. He thanked her for calling him. Everyone got in and they were off.

Alex realized that she was hurting more than she expected. She figured it was a delayed reaction or that she was finally paying attention. She relaxed and listened to the flow of the conversation of the other three.

They arrived at Annie's house and were in the process of getting out of the taxi when a person approached and in an authoritative voice introduced himself as the lawyer for Jeff Thomas's parents.

Alex was surprised as her mother replied in an equally strong authoritative voice that she was the lawyer for the Scots and for Ms. Evercrest and asked what he had in mind.

Her mother's reply seemed to take the steam out of the person and in a much quieter voice and a changed attitude he handed her a paper that he said required them to attend child custody court hearing a week from now on the subject of custody of the two children.

Alex's mother replied that she would accept the request but that she had a court order calling his clients to attend court in Chicago to prove their fitness to raise the girls and that the appearance was set for noon on Tuesday.

There was a moment of silence as the person seemed to assess the situation. He then said that the timing was inconvenient and interfered with the timing that was in the document he had presented.

Alex's mother replied that it did not matter. The timing in Chicago was set. Missing that would land his two clients in jail. She went on to hand him another envelope and told him to study his client's background. Perhaps he could convince them that they did not stand a chance.

Her mother then told him that would be all.

Alex was amaze when the person turned and walked back to his car. It was clear that her mother metaphorically had more or less wacked him alongside of the head.

Alex quietly thanked her for the show of force.

Her mother smiled and said that would slow the charge. She said that she was sure that the lawyer in question would most likely be surprised by his client's background and would most likely discourage them from going forward.

Then she laughed and said if they showed up in court in Chicago, they would spend the day only to find out they were not on the docket. I sent a message to my judge friend who is presiding, to let him know about the situation and asked him to have his clerk make the two sit and cool their heels before letting them know there was some mistake, and the court would get back to them if their presence was required.

She turned and led the way up the walk to the porch to the front door and rang the bell.

Alex got the hugs she had been looking forward to. She introduced everyone and then she held Linda and Laurie by the hand and was led in.

They were the first. It had been planned that way. Her mother called Linda and Laurie to her and presented them with the teddy bears. She made a point to let them know that she had given one to Alex when she was their age and she still had hers on her bed.

After some oohing and hugging of the bears they ran out of the room saying they were going to put them on their beds.

Annie had tears in her eyes as she thanked Alex's mother.

After a brief moment, the bottles of wine and the flowers were presented to Annie's mother.

Matt received a hug from Linda for having thought of her and brought her flowers.

She made the point that her granddaughter could be called little Linda, but she would not tolerate being called "big or old" Linda. That got a rise from everyone.

Alex presented her gift and Annie once again had tears in her eyes. She looked at Alex and told her that she would not accept it unless Alex accepted another painting. Alex smiled and responded that she had been hoping she would be lucky enough to be able to hang several of Annie's paintings in her apartment. They hugged and the deal was sealed.

Annie and Alex's mother went to the next room.

The doorbell rang and Brenda, the art dealer and her husband were at the door.

Linda declared that dinner would be served in the kitchen by the catering crew. There were drinks of choice available from beer to whiskey. She went on to say that seating would be anywhere in the house or back porch.

Alex could hear Annie's exclamation, "You did that. Is it legal to send them to Chicago to appear in court?" Then there was laughter and Annie's follow up comment, "now I know where Alex got her drive for action."

Alex's drive for action was a strength that came at a price that had a boom-a-rang associated with it. In the near future it would have an unexpected consequence. It was a consequence that she would later realize was her continuing interaction with the hand from above.

15 The Meaning of Survival

The arrival of Sheriff Evan and his wife was followed by the arrival of the Chief and his wife. The two couples were both introduced and were soon sitting near each other discussing the current case.

Their discussion focused heavily on Alex.

When Trey arrived, Alex made the point of introducing Nolan to Linda and Laurie.

Annie greeted Nolan by name and then took the three down into the basement. She was followed by one of the two caterers with a helping of food for each. Annie had set up a small table for the three to share. She said they could have seconds and when they were done, they should put their paper plates and silverware in the trash can. Then they could have dessert

Afterwards they should decide which board game to play. She let Linda and Laurie know that it was a special night and bedtime would be when Nolan left.

The three immediately dug into the food and Annie turned and went back upstairs.

She approached Trey and Leslie and told them that Nolan was a handsome and well-behaved son. Then she excused herself and went and got a plate of food and returned to chat with them about schooling and how they took care of Nolan. She asked what Nolan did during the day. She wanted to know if he was allowed to go out around the neighborhood on his own.

Lesley said that she did not let him go out on his own even if he was going to be with other kids. Either she or Trey were always present but stayed in the background.

Alex was sitting not far away and listened into parts of the conversation. She knew that Leslie worked part-time but was always at home with Nolan. She dropped him off at daycare and then went to work. She left work and picked Nolan up and went home where she prepared a snack and then prepared dinner.

She realized that the discussion was very helpful in getting Annie on her road to navigating life outside the cabin where she had been held for most of her life.

The dinner and discussion flowed smoothly into early evening. Alex chatted with everyone, but she was especially interested in how her mother and Annie got along. It was clear that Annie was asking many questions that her mother seemed to answer without hesitation. Alex had given her mother the research into Jeff's parents and knew that her mother would carry the day in any court that might handle the case.

Alex relaxed in the comfortable easy chair. She must have dosed off because Matt nudged her and asked if she had enough for the evening.

Her arm wound was throbbing, and her chest ached, and she was exhausted but the glow of having solved the long cold case still carried the day.

The dinner had capped the event for Alex.

Sheriff Evan came over and congratulated her on having solved the cold case and thanked her for taking the albatross from around his neck.

Alex replied that they had all contributed to its resolution. She called Johnnie over and highlighted his contribution. She recognized Trey for having saved her life. She jokingly recognized the Chief for supplying her with an endless supply of cars to get blown up as needed.

She took out the picture of Annie's parents in front of the fireplace and told everyone that it had been the picture that immediately calmed Annie down and allowed her to react to Jeff's attack.

She went and stood by Annie and gave her a hug and pointed out that Annie had demonstrated what surviving meant. She was an inspiration that had developed herself in the face of being a chained captive.

She then proposed a toast to living well in the future and watching the three kids in the basement as they grew up.

After the toast Alex thanked Annie and her mother for the great time and bade everyone a good night.

She led the way out to the waiting taxi.

She was looking forward to the weekend and a couple of days to let it all unwind.

The next morning, she had her now favorite taxi driver take her mother to the airport.

She then decided to take her bike ride east along the river. She biked at an easy relaxed pace and thought through everything that had happened.

The actions of Jeff's parents were the only pieces of the puzzle that seemed to leave a hole in the picture. Why would they want to try to get two small children at this stage of their lives? It made little sense.

Her left arm was letting her know that it was at its limit. When she got back, she decided to walk her bike up from the river front. As she walked up the slight hill, she noticed a large black pickup with Idaho license plates on the truck.

Her intuition set alarm bells off in her head.

The truck passenger door suddenly opened and a woman with a gun in her hand stepped out and aimed it at her. She began by calling Alex rude names and cursing.

Alex was unarmed but with all her strength, she launched her bike at the woman and followed behind it and grabbed the woman by the wrist that held the gun.

The gun fired and Alex felt the bullet hit her right shoulder. She twisted the gun up under the woman's chin and pushed on her trigger finger.

She knew the woman was dead. She struggled to hold the woman up as she stumbled back under the weight and stepped on her bike and slowly felt back over it.

She grabbed the gun as they fell.

She saw the driver raise what appeared to be a shotgun. She fired twice and was launched backward by the impact of the shotgun blast.

Both she and the woman were launched several feet beyond her fallen bike.

As the world around her dimmed she hoped they were both dead. She figured she might be and if the shooter with the shot gun survived, she was sure she was dead.

The world went blank. She did not hear the wailing of the rescue unit. She did not feel the shot to her arm meant to help her survive. She did not hear Matt tell her to hold on.

Her mind rambled in unexpected directions. There seemed to be voices and singing. She was talking to someone that she thought she knew. He was thanking her for having solved his case. There were two women cursing her. She was reminded by Professor Sievert that she should be figuring out what she wanted to do in the future.

Alex was totally confused. She struggled to wake up.

Finally, she was able to open her eyes. The first person she saw when she opened her eyes was her mother and standing next to her was Matt.

She looked at her mother and asked her where she was. Then Alex recalled that she had sent her off to the airport on the way back to Chicago.

She asked if she was alive or dreaming.

Her mother replied that she was in the hospital and that she was alive..

Her mother explained that she had just landed in Chicago when she got a call from the Chief to let her know that had been shot and were in the hospital.

She had gotten on the next flight back to Cincinnati.

Alex reached out and gave her mother's hand a squeeze and thanked her.

Matt was still his uniform.

She then asked which hospital she was in.

Matt told her that he and his team had been the ones to bring her to the hospital. He went on to tell her that she had been shot through the shoulder by a thirty-eight-caliber bullet. He rattled a small glass jar that held a slightly deformed slug. Lucky for her it missed all vital organs and lodged in the muscle of her back.

The surgeons had removed the bullet from her back and had closed the bullet hole just above her right breast.

He emphasized that a hearse had picked up the two people she had shot. The shotgun blast had almost severed the woman in two and Alex had been hit by only one pellet alongside of her hip. He held up a second small glass jar and rattled it.

He handed both plastic jars to Trey who was standing at the end of the bed

The doctor who arrived as Alex was coming out of a drugged state said that the impact of hitting the ground had most likely been the reason she had blacked out. She had been checked for a concussion but seemed not to have sustained one. The doctor figured that she was suffering from the accumulated trauma that she had experienced during the last couple of weeks.

She commented that Alex would have a small scar on her back but that it would not be very noticeable. She told her how lucky she had been that the bullet went between two ribs and stopped in her back muscle and did not tear a hole out the back.

She then said that the pellet in her hip that must have come through the woman she was holding did not do much damage.

Alex smiled and commented that yes, she was indeed a lucky person. She was always surviving what was trying to kill her.

Johnnie walked in and told her she had made the news and that there was a slew of local and national reporters eager to talk to her.

The Chief came in next and asked how she was feeling. He put up his hand and commented that he could not even give her time off without there being a gun battle.

Alex then said that it would have been a lot easier if she had been armed.

She then asked him if he would mind dealing with the reporters.

The Chief smiled and said he would take care of the folks in the waiting area. He looked at the doctor and asked if he would like to make the national news.

Alex smiled as the two turned and walked out together as they strategized on what to say.

She was surprised when Annie walked in and leaned in to give her a hug. She had tears in her eyes and was having trouble talking as she again thanked Alex. She said that she could not believe that Jeff's parents had tried to kill her.

Alex was about to reply, when Annie stepped back and put her arms around, Alex mother's shoulders and said that she had been assured by her that she would never see Jeff's parents in court, but she had not expected her to tell Alex to go and take them out.

Her mother looked at Annie for a moment and then chuckled and said, "you were found by the right woman, she isn't called Cincinnati's Black Annie Oakley for nothing."

16 Future

Alex was in the hospital for a solid week.** She was out of bed and walking on the morning following her surgery.

Matt made it a point to come in during his lunch break and either have lunch with her or walk the halls with her.

Her doctor complemented her on doing the walking, but she let Alec know that she would not release her until she had fully recovered. She wanted her bruises from the car bomb blast to get a chance to heal. She wanted the wounds in her shoulder and arm to heal before she would sign a release.

Her mother called every morning to chat.

Annie came in each day to share a cup of coffee.

Johnnie, Trey, Bill, and Trevor came in together about every other day.

Annie arrived in the middle of the week with a huge smile and said she had great news.

She let Alex know that she and Brenda had opened up a day-care center next to Brenda's art supply and studio. Brenda had cleared one of the storage rooms and turned into an art studio.

This meant that Linda and Laurie had a place adjacent to her new studio where she was planning to continue to paint.

Having my own art studio had been one of her dreams while she had been chained in the woods.

She then shared that there would be a showing that would be hosted by Cincinnati Art Museum. It would get local, national, and international coverage. She said that Brenda was really great to work with, and her associate was very eager to work with her.

Brenda's associate was handling an auction of some of her works. He claimed that the first auction would most likely net several million dollars.

He and Brenda had drafted a contract that she had sent to Alex's mother for review and editing that spelled out the terms of the handling of her paintings.

Brenda's associate claimed that the first auction would most likely net several million dollars.

She added that she had put in an application to three universities in the area and would evaluate them based on which university gave her the most credits for the self-study that she had done.

The final piece of news was that Brenda had scheduled a private showing. She had been the one to decide who would attend. She handed Alex the invitation letter and a list of all the names of those that were invited for a private showing.

She had included some of her childhood school friends a couple of her teachers and all the people that were involved with rescuing her.

One name stood out on the list to Alex, Rob Netherland. She pointed to it and asked about him.

Annie smiled and replied that he had been her best friend when she was a girl. He claimed that he had thought of her every day since the day she was abducted.

He had attended the opening of the day care center and had taken her to lunch. It was clear that they were on the way to being more than friends.

She looked at Alex and thanked her for calling Rob to make sure he was at her house to greet her. Her match making seemed to be working. She said that she hoped the match making moved at an Alex Evercrest speed and that it would last a lifetime. She would let Alex know it that happened.

Alex's doctor came in and asked if the two of them were ready to leave the hospital.

Alex was caught by surprise. She looked at Annie and realized that Annie was beaming a smile.

Annie said, "There is a special group of people that are waiting outside to see you to your favorite cab. One of them is Matt, one of them is Rob and the other two are Brenda and her husband."

We are all having lunch at Scoto's. They are featuring my paintings and are hosting the lunch free of charge.

When Alex walked into Scoto's she realized that Annie had invited all of the detective teams that had been part of rescuing her. Sheriff Williams had a huge smile as he gave her a hug.

The Chief handed her the keys to a new car and said he expected her for work on Monday.

The End

Preview of: Maggot

Maggot

1 Captives

She was shoved roughly into a high-backed chair. She felt her wrists being secured to the chair side rails. When the hood was removed from her head, Alex took note of the large one-foot wide square, hand hewn beams supporting the barn floor above her. It was the signature of a barn at least one hundred years old. The only clue as to her location was that it had taken only a few minutes from the time she and Trey had been run off the road and captured to the time their abductors removed her hood.

Trey was standing still hooded and what followed made Alex sick to her stomach. Trey had his hands tied behind his back. The largest of the three thugs pulled the hood off, stood before Trey, and told him that his name was Brutus. He said that if Trey didn't answer his questions, he would enjoy slowly beating him to death.

The second person said his name was Mad Sam and he was going to enjoy helping Brutus.

The two of them looked over at the third person and said his name was Larry and that Larry was the boss's personal cameraman.

Then Brutus delivered the first of what seemed and endless flow of punches to Trey's mid-section. Each punch drove Trey back a step.

Nothing escaped Trey's mouth but the flow of air. Alex cringed each time Trey was punched. Both Brutus and Mad Sam seemed to get angrier and angrier with each punch.

Then they knocked Trey off his feet and proceeded to kick him in the stomach and back. They stood Trey up again and punched him in the face. Each hit was delivered with mind numbing brute force.

Larry was using his phone in the video mode. He would move close in to capture punches and kicks. He might not be doing the punching, but Alex saw that he was enjoying creating the video.

She could not believe the strength of character that Trey was demonstrating. After having been kicked repeatedly when he fell, after he was hit in the face by the huge hulk that laughed every time, he delivered a blow, Trey finally fell to his knees and hung his head in resignation.

To Alex, Trey seemed to have passed out in the kneeling position.

Blood was running from his mouth and nose, and one eye was swollen shut. He had his hands tied behind his back and had been helpless as he was punched in his torso and face and kicked in the ribs.

Each time he fell down he was repeatedly kicked. His two assailants were enjoying themselves as they asked Trey what he knew about their distribution operation.

The cameraman, as Alex thought of Larry, walked around getting his pictures. It was clear to Alex he was treating the action like a movie scene.

Trey had never said a word or reacted to the brutal beating he was taking. His passive behavior and total silence seemed to infuriate both of his brutalizers.

She was sure someone on the statewide drug eradication team had ratted them out. If she lived, she would find out who and make sure that person paid for their disloyalty to the police force.

Just when it seemed that the thugs were getting ready to shoot both of them a voice from outside of the barn yelled that the boss wanted to speak to all of them.

The instant the three thugs walked out and closed the barn door Alex acted.

She rocked her chair until it fell on its right side. The right arm rest broke when the chair hit the cement floor.

At first, she thought she might have broken her arm or her shoulder. She knew she didn't have time to worry about any injuries.

She used the sharp broken end of the arm rest to cut the tape on her left arm. Then she freed her right arm and then used the arm rest to tear the tape holding her feet.

Trey had not moved and was still in his kneeling position with his head bent forward. He looked like a supplicant kneeling to a king.

Alex nudged him and whispered his name. He seemed to come awake. Alex helped him stand and supported him as she led him toward the back of the barn.

She had to get them as far away as possible.

She opened a regular sized door to the side of the larger sliding door. As she opened it slowly, she thanked the farmer for keeping the hinges well oiled. It opened silently.

Alex took a quick look around and decided that the forest just beyond the barn fence would be their best chance at eluding their captures.

As they walked toward the forest it was clear to her that Trey would not make it far. She was the only thing that was keeping him upright. She knew that escape through the forest was out of the question, but she figured it was the only place to take Trey.

Just inside the forest she saw a huge tree that had fallen over. Last fall's leaves had filled the large depression where the roots had pulled out of the ground. She guided Trey and walked him into the depression. She realized the leaves were floating over a large puddle of water.

She knew she would have to be fast in getting him out of the cold water, but she had no choice but to put him into the depression and cover him with leaves.

She told him to breath softly and not to move. She was not sure he heard her. She knew she had to move quickly and get away from him. She needed her captures to chase her and not look for Trey.

She backtracked a short distance to the edge of the forest and waited for the thugs. They were now yelling about the escape. They were pointing to the woods, and she could hear the person in the lead yelling, "this way."

She wanted them to follow her as she ran in a wide circle that would lead them away from where she had left Trey. She planned to get back to the front of the barn.

She had decided to be the hunter and not the hunted.

The broken arm of the chair was her only weapon. The arm was much lighter in weight and could not be used quite as effectively as a police baton, but she planned to use it more like a hand spear and thrust it into her victim's gut or throat.

It was a simple plan. Move fast, spread out the three thugs and disable or kill them one at a time. She planned to use any means possible, but she figured her chances were slim and she would probably end up dead.

She moved out running as fast as she could manage. She was seen almost immediately, and the thugs took her bait and began shooting at her. She zigged and zagged but ran in a large circle back toward the barn.

She heard the shots, but she was not hit, and she did not stop. She figured her speed and the fact that the thugs were shooting on the run was the only reason she was still alive. She was still concerned about some random slug taking her down.

As she cleared the corner of the barn, she came face to face with the fourth person that had stayed with the car. His surprised look signaled that he had not expected her, but he was quickly reaching for his gun.

Alex continued her running while lifting her right arm that held the arm rest. She used all her strength and momentum and drove the point of the chair arm through his throat. There was enough force to drive it all the way through his neck. He died instantly.

She picked up his gun just in time to confront the fastest of the three pursuers as he rounded the corner of the barn.

It was Brutus and the look on his face as Alex pulled the trigger was all the reward she would need. The small hole between his eyes belied the fact that the back of his head was missing. Later she would recall the sound of white brain matter splattering across the side of the barn and see the fresco it had created.

Alex immediately moved behind the car.

The next two thugs rounded the corner of the barn and stopped in their tracks. They were looking at the two bodies of their peers. One was lying in a large pool of blood with the chair handle through his throat and the other with the back of his head missing.

Alex called out for them to drop their guns and surrender. Mad Sam lifted his gun to shoot, and Larry's eyes bulged as he took in the white matter of two brains that had created brain matter art. He was tempted to get a picture for the boss, but he immediately put his hands in the air and yelled out that he surrendered.

He could not get the image of the white brain matter splattered across the red barn out of his mind.

He watched the black detective walk toward him.

Alex shot him in the leg that he had used to kick Trey. She thought about adding his brains to the "brain matter barn art" that she had created but she needed him alive.

She wanted the name of his boss.

She told him to stand up and walk slowly into the barn. She told him that he would die instantly if he tried anything at all. She zip-tied his hand behind his back and made him kneel. She kicked him in the leg that she had just shot. She then used duct tape as a tourniquet to stop the flow of blood from his leg. She taped his feet together. And then taped his mouth shut.

She stepped in front of him and told him she would be right back and that he should not move.

She exited the barn and found the car keys in the pocket of the first person she had killed. She also found his cell phone and put in a call to 911. She identified herself and told the person that answered that she had just shot four people and that she would leave the phone on so that it would provide the police the location of where she was.

The operator started to ask a series of questions. Alex told her to stop and contact the police and to send out an ambulance. She put the phone on the ground next to the three bodies. She got into the car and drove across the field to get the car as close to Trey as she could. She left the car on and the heater going full blast.

Trey had come around and regained consciousness. He did not know where he was and at first thought he was in Iraq. Then he realized that he was laying in wet mud and water. There was no sand in his mouth and no sun burning his brains to a crisp. His head was propped up but covered with leaves. He was not sure what was going on, but he faintly remembered Alex helping him out of the barn. He was freezing and his body was numb. He was beyond shivering.

He very slowly lifted his right hand to his face and took off a few leaves.

He was surprised to see Alex walking swiftly toward him.

He knew immediately a miracle had happened.

Alex had somehow taken control of the situation.

He wondered if there were any survivors.

Alex looked down at him and reached her hand down to help him get up out of the mud and water.

She could feel Trey start to shiver and knew he was close to hypothermia. She put his right arm over her shoulder and together they slowly walked to the car. She helped him into the right front seat. She got into the driver's side and drove slowly back to the front of the barn.

She watched as Trey clumsily adjusted the vents. He held his shivering hands, one on each of the vents. She had never felt so relieved as she did at this moment.

Both of them had survived.

Trey was a beaten mess, but she knew he had the will and the strength to survive.

It was hard for her to look at his face.

She heard the sirens and could see the approaching flashing lights across the field.

Alex parked the car next to the barn.

She told Trey to relax and wait for the EMT's.

She then walked into the barn and pulled the tape off Larry's mouth. She asked if he could hear the police sirens. When he said that yes, he could, she told him that she was inclined to shoot him in the head and add his brain matter to the side of the barn.

He had to the count of three to tell her the name of the person who had called and where he was located otherwise the sound of his approaching rescue would be the last sound, he heard.

Larry hesitated. Alex kicked him in his injured leg again as she pulled back the guns action as if to chamber a bullet. She then put the gun to his forehead and simply said one.

She immediately got her answer.

She stepped out in front of him and smiled and said that she had lied. She seemed to hesitate for a moment then put the gun to his forehead and pulled the trigger. The hammer fell on an empty chamber, but the loud click had done its job.

The front of the Larry's pants revealed his reaction.

She walked out of the barn and put all the weapons in a pile.

She checked to see that Trey was OK. He had passed out, but he was breathing evenly.

She went to the front of the car and waited.

Three police cars with flashing lights and one ambulance rapidly approached.

Alex stood with her arms raised.

She identified herself and Trey. She asked the paramedics to immediately attend to Trey. She then told the deputy about the captive in the barn, and she pointed to the three bodies and informed him that they had resisted arrest.

She had survived. She now planned to hunt for the maggot that had betrayed them, and she intended to get the boss that had instructed the thugs to beat the information out of Trey and her.

She watched the EMT's remove Trey from the car. They put him on a back board and removed his wet clothes. The bruises on his torso were already showing. She heard one of the EMT's confirm what she had suspected when Trey had moaned at each step that she had helped him take. One EMT looked over at her and told her Trey had at least two broken ribs.

Trey had his eyes closed but was breathing in a steady rhythm. Alex wondered what they were waiting on when she heard the sound of a helicopter.

One of the EMT's came over to her and let her know that they were having the helicopter take Trey to the VA hospital. They had found his instructions to do so in his wallet. She said Trey would recover.

She added that Trey was one of the more brutally beaten persons that her team had ever attended to. She finished by letting Alex know that he had been given a sedative and he was resting peacefully.

Alex wanted to go with Trey but knew she had to stay. She watched his stretcher being covered with a thermal blanket and strapped onto the rescue helicopter.

She let out a sigh of relief. She had almost lost a close friend and the best partner on the force. She would check in on his condition as soon as she could.

The EMT's came over and quickly checked her out. She had one long scratch on her leg that she had inflicted when she was getting her leg free of the chair but otherwise, she had come through with no other injuries.

Next the EMT's attended to Larry who was strapped on a back board and placed in the ambulance. He loudly complained about being assaulted by a police officer but stopped when one of the deputies told him that he would have his mouth taped shut if he continued.

An entire evidence picture taking crew arrived a short time later.

Alex had explained the situation several times to the senior deputy in charge. She was getting tired of the request to explain again how she and Trey had ended up in the barn.

The deputy pointed out that she was well out of her jurisdiction.

He wanted to know how she had been able to overcome four well-armed men.

She did not bring up the fact that the thugs had underestimated and ignored her and focused on Trey. This had given her a slim chance at survival. She had played the hand that she was dealt. Their underestimation of her as an adversary had cost three of them their lives. She wished she would have had the gumption to shoot Larry in the head. He so deserved to be on the pile with the other three.

The backdrop of the sun behind the tall slowly waving corn stalks made them seem to Alex like a million swords waving in the wind. She thought her interpretation was appropriate and supported the fury she had running through her mind.

Alex watched a familiar Cincinnati Police helicopter approach and land. The Chief, Trevor and Bill got out and walked toward her.

She was glad to see them. She knew the Chief would now take the lead in communicating with the Sheriff.

She was not sure how she would do it, but she was going to take the battle, which had been triggered by the cartel's decision to abduct her and Trey, to the very top of the drug hierarchy. She mentally cast herself into the role of the avenging angel.

Only later would she learn the significance of that thought.

2 The Chief

*T*he call from the Washington Courthouse Sheriff had caught him by surprise. Bruce Johnson, Chief of the Cincinnati Detective group, stood up and paced as he listened to the Sheriff ask him about an Alex Evercrest, who claimed to work for him. He was surprised about the details of the crime scene and knew by the description of the condition of the three dead men that it was Alex that had done the shooting.

He was more disturbed when the sheriff described the physical condition of a Trey McGregor. It was clear to Bruce that Alex's action had been to protect Trey and herself. He told the sheriff not to move anything at the crime scene he would be up as quickly as possible.

He said he and a couple of his other detectives would be up to examine the scene and that he would appreciate having the crime scene left as it had been found. He wanted to get a sense of what had occurred.

He told the sheriff to treat Alex with kid gloves and that she was one of his best detectives and was assigned to the Ohio State's drug eradication team and that he was sure that the situation was related to the drug trade.

After having gotten the Sheriff's assurance, he walked out of his office and over to Bill and Travis's area and told them that Alex and Trey had been abducted and that somehow Alex had freed herself and Trey. He said he wanted them to accompany him to the Washington Courthouse area and examine the crime scene.

Travis asked if any of the perpetrators were still alive.

Bruce was about to lead the way to his car when Bill commented that perhaps they should check on the availability of one of the department helicopters.

It sounded like a good idea to Bruce. It would reduce the travel time by a good thirty minutes and would keep him from driving like a maniac.

As the three walked out to the waiting hilo, Travis commented that in his book Bill had just earned a gold star. He would share that with Alex and see if he could get them a couple of her delicious cookies.

The Chief looked at Travis and said that he better wait a few days before approaching Alex or teasing her. She had just eliminated three tough drug thugs for beating Trey and was probably not in a kidding mood.

On the way he shared what he had learned about the situation. Bill listened and only let out a quiet whistle and a wow. Travis, who always gave Alex a hard time, commented that her capturers had made a big mistake in making her mad. Now that he understood what she had gone through he agreed that it would be best to leave the teasing for another time. He went on to say that the parties responsible for Trey's beating had no clue of the tempest they had unleashed.

The chopper pilot pointed to a burning auto as they neared the coordinates he had been given.

Travis bet it was Alex's new car.

The Chief gave a small groan and asked the pilot to briefly touch down and let him talk to the firemen.

The lead fireman came over and the Chief showed him his badge. He commented that he thought the car was one of his.

The fireman paused and then turned around and went back to the fire truck and reached inside. He came back with two phones and asked if the phones were official police issue. He said the phones had been found in the grass by the fence.

He went on to say that his crew guessed that they had been thrown there intentionally because they were both on.

Bill dialed Alex's number and the black phone in the Chief's hand rang. Travis dialed Trey's phone and the other phone rang.

The fireman nodded as the rings answered his question about the ownership of the phones. He pointed to the car and said that it would be taken to the junk yard once the sheriff cleared its removal. Meanwhile until it cooled, the sheriff had assigned one of the junior deputies to guard it. Then it would be taken to the evidence lot.

The Chief handed the phones to Travis. He led the way back to the chopper.

He wondered how he would be able to get another car. Alex was three for three, three cases, three cars destroyed.

In less than a minute they were landing near the red barn.

Three police cars and a third black automobile were in front of the barn. Alex was sitting on the hood of the black car.

It was no surprise to Bruce that she looked worn out. She and Trey had left the office earlier in the morning on the way to investigate a lead that had been given them by their team. He was not aware where they were headed but had wished them well. Now he wished he was more involved in what they were doing.

Travis got out of the chopper and walked toward Alex. It was only noon, but it was clear to him that she was stressed. He said hello and handed her phone to her.

She thanked him and asked about her car.

Travis replied that it had seen better days and was on its way to be flattened and recycled.

Travis passed up the chance to rib her about her brand-new car that she had for less than a month but was now a burned-out skeleton. The previous car issued to Alex had been blown up during her last case. He would wait until a much later date to rib her about her luck with cars.

Instead, he asked about Trey.

Alex replied that she had never seen anyone as brave, as resilient and able to survive the brutal beating that he had experienced. She said that she was in hell's limbo as she waited to hear how he was doing.

He listened as the Chief asked if she was alright.

Alex replied that she was better than alright. She was alive.

Then Bruce asked what hospital Trey was taken to. He was at first surprised that Trey had specified the VA but then he remembered that Trey was a veteran of the last two wars that the US had been in and had been decorated for his bravery in battle.

He looked over at Bill and asked him to call the VA medical center and find out Trey's condition.

Then Bruce looked at Travis and asked him to arrange to have all the pictures that had already been taken sent to the Cincinnati office. He wanted them in electronic format. No paper copies.

He stood looking at the brain splatter on the side of the barn. Alex was a dead shot. She was known in the department as "Cincinnati's Black Annie Oakley" and he figured she was at least that good. She not only could shoot but she moved fast, and she was deadly with or without a gun.

He examined the three bodies and realized that one of them had met his maker by having the broken end of an armchair driven through his throat and having his spine split in two. Alex had to have been remarkably close to have used the armchair in that manner. He wanted to ask her, but he figured that she must have surprised him and killed him first. The second one had to be the huge monster because the third body was on top of him.

The brain splatter on the side of the red barn was a first for him. He stood back and was shocked that to him it seemed to be quite beautiful. He controlled his urge to take a picture of it.

He looked over to where Alex was talking on her phone. She was petite but as the three thugs on the ground learned in the ultimate way, she was deadly.

He wondered who she was talking to.

He went inside the barn.

He walked over to the broken chair that marked the location from where Alex had witnessed Trey's beating. He stood looking at the blood splatter that covered the cement floor. The amount of blood clearly evoked the vision in his mind of a brutal beating. He wondered about the quantity of blood that Trey had lost.

He wondered how Alex had taken it. He had seen what he thought was a bruise on the side of her face and figured she had voiced her anger.

The coroner was still working the scene, so he walked over and asked. He was told that it was probably a pint of blood that was splattered across the floor. The coroner went on to say that a person with that much blood loss usually had so many internal injuries that they were unlikely to survive.

Bruce figured it was a miracle that Trey and Alex were both alive. He was now counting on the doctors and Trey to come through and prove the coroner wrong.

But he knew it was a miracle that was only made possible by the tenacious attitude of his "Annie Oakley."

He followed one of the sheriff's men to the woods to the location at the end of a huge fallen tree. He would have missed where Alex had hidden Trey if he had not been shown the spot. She had put Trey in the one place where she could leave him hidden well enough that she could go on the attack unhindered by her brutally beaten partner.

He was then taken along the circular path Alex had run as she was being shot at. A large number of slugs had been found by a crew working the area with metal detectors. They figured that the twenty-five recovered slugs were probably a small portion of the number that had been fired.

Bruce shook his head as he thought about Alex's actions. Her first concern had been to protect Trey, and her second action was to set up a situation where she had a chance to take control.

Under fire by her pursuers, she went on the attack with no weapon other than a broken armchair handle. She willingly ran a gauntlet of gunfire as she launched her attack. He was sure the three chasing her never had a clue that she was not running but attacking them by setting them up and spreading them out.

He could now see that she had figured on eliminating them one at a time.

He knew he would never be able to publicly recognize Alex for her bravery, but the department would know, and he would share it up the chain of command. She had demonstrated bravery beyond the call of duty. She deserved to be recognized. He would clearly put it in her service record.

His deputy guide brought him around the barn to the three dead bodies.

The coroner looked up at him and commented that he had never worked such a bizarre scene.

Bruce found himself standing in front of Alex.

He walked up to her and gave her a hug and told her that her tenacity and bravery was an inspiration to him and to the entire police department.

Bill and Travis were standing at the open barn door.

Bill looked over to where the Chief was standing and in an uncharacteristic comment said that "Our Annie Oakley" displayed more than just shooting ability. She has truly displayed unequaled courage and how deadly she is in hand-to-hand, person-to-person combat.

Bruce looked at Bill and agreed. He then said that it was time for all of them to get back to Cincinnati.

He signaled the chopper pilot and led the way. Alex put away her phone and followed the three of them. She strapped on her seat belt and put on the earphones the pilot handed to her.

She put them on, entered a quiet environment, and heard the pilot explain that the headphones suppressed the noise and allowed for almost normal conversation.

Alex told the Chief that her weapon and Trey's were in the Washington Court House Sheriff's possession and were evidence in a crime scene.

She asked if there was anything anyone wanted to know about what had happened at the crime scene.

Bruce asked about the fourth thug that had survived. He said that the sheriff had told him that the thug was complaining about police brutality.

Alex replied that the thug was named Larry, and he had been the camera man during the beating.

He was still alive because he had cooperated after being wounded by a stray shot from one of his companion's gun. She did not mention that the gun was in her hand and that her bullets did not stray.

The Chief knew better than to ask.

Alex explained that Larry had sent the video that he made of the beating to his boss. Alex held out an I-phone and handed it to the Chief.

She said Johnnie needed to have the e-mail address and the I-phone number of the person the message was sent to. She asked that the video be put into the official police file but that it be kept out of the news.

She looked at the chief and asked him to seal and archive the phone and video for at least ten years.

Alex then told the chief that she planned on visiting some friends that lived in the east and would be gone for a few days.

Then afterward she planned to go fishing in Lake Michigan with Matt and be gone for another week.

Bruce agreed to archive the phone after Johnnie was through with it. He reminded her that even though he was putting her on active duty leave for the next several weeks she was still on the force and her duty was to enforce and uphold the law.

Alex turned to look over her shoulder and replied that she planned to do just that.

Bruce knew she would go to the edge but not cross the line, but little did he know that the edge would sweep back and forth more like the tail of an attacking alligator than the straight line of the law as he was imagining it.

Thank you for reading this far.

To continue reading **Maggot** go to

https://www.Remwriter95.net/

<u>About the Author</u>

Ronald E. Mueller
remwriter95@gmail.com

Ron grew up in what is now Flint River State Park in Southeast Iowa. The 170-year-old house Ron lived in is built into a hillside. It faces a 125-foot-high cliff towering over the little Flint River. The house and the land talked to him about; the passing of time, the struggle to conquer the land, the struggles people faced and the wonder of nature.

He climbed the cliffs, crawled into the caves, dove from the swimming rock, collected clams from the bottom of the pond, gigged and skinned frogs for their legs. He trapped muskrats for fur, hunted raccoon in the dead of night, and with only a stick hunted rabbits in the dead of winter.

His young life was outdoors, and nature tested him.

He walked to a one room stone schoolhouse uphill both ways. A stern but warm-hearted teacher, Mrs. Henry was instrumental in shaping his character as she shepherded him from the fourth to the eighth grade.

It was a great way to grow up.

Ron graduated from Burlington, High School, went to Vietnam in the Navy. He graduated from The University of South Florida with an master's degree in engineering, worked for thirty eight years for Procter and Gamble, traveled around the world thirty times.

He has remained happily married for more than fifty years. His daughter and his two sons are all successful and his three grandchildren have all graduated.

His wife has humored and supported him as he became a full time professional story teller.

He has come to realize that he is, what is known as, a Cozy writer. Excitement and adventure but little guts and gore. His heroine or hero live happily ever after.

His experiences inter-twined with snippets of fantasy lend themselves to the adventures he leads the reader through.

Books by Ron Mueller

Fiction Series
The Alex Evercrest Series
The River Front
The Girl on The Grill
Missing
Maggot
Racist
Votive Candles
Windy City
Country Road
Pool of Blood
Sins of the Daughter
Body Parts
The Skull Collector
The Vanishing
The Shadow Fighter
Moonshine
Grief's Trajectory
The Magic Touch
Northern Lights
Alex Evercrest Heroine
Alex Evercrest Collection Two
New Direction
A Family Affair
Disruption
The St. Lebuinnus Church Murder

A Brian O'Neil Novel
Hawaiian Phoenix
Moon Curser
Death Broker

The Problem Solver Series
Solutions
Drug Lords
Border Crosser
The Problem Solver Collection

The Taelo Series
Taelo: The Early Years
Taelo: The Golden Feather
Taelo: Journey of Discovery
Taelo: Dangerous Passage
Taelo: Condor Clan Slingers
Taelo: Circumvention
Taelo: The Journey of Sages
Taelo: Collection
Taelo: Future Leaders Journey

A Taelo Story:
White Swan and Quiet Pheasant
The Child's Name
Floating Cloud
Quiet Rabbit

Busy Bee
Little Otter & Talking Wren
Broken Spear
Burley Bear & Meadow Flower
Taelo Story Collection

Science Fiction

The Savitar Series:
Journey's End
Savitar
Confluence
Savitar Series Collection

Bram Nielson Series
The Fold
The Message
Fold Wormhole
Negative Fold
Ripples in Time
Bram Nielson Collection

Single Science Fiction Books:
Current Past and Future
The Event
The Door
Viajante 7

Published by: Around the World Publishing LLC.

https://www.Remwriter95.net/